Dear readers,

Bat-confession: Last summer, when I first realized that Greg Capullo and I were going to end our five-year run on BATMAN, I had no idea what to do next. I ended up doing some real soul-searching. I considered taking a new character, or doing a graphic novel. To be honest, I even considered leaving superhero comics for a bit... After all, that run, from BATMAN #1 through BATMAN #51, had been the ride of my life. I knew it then and I know it now. When I started it, I was a new name, still green from the book world, and abjectly terrified... And while I'm still abjectly terrified most of the time, I'm a more confident writer now; I know myself better. I grew up on Batman, as did Greg, and my hope is that some of the success of the book had to do with everyone who read it feeling like they were watching two creators grow together, as individuals and as partners. When we started, Greg and I didn't get along at all. Now, our families take vacations together–he's a big brother to me. So continue without him? It didn't seem possible.

But then I started thinking about the stories I hadn't really had a chance to tell yet, the characters I hadn't gotten to write...So many of the greats: Two-Face, Poison Ivy, Penguin, Mad Hatter. And I also started thinking about the other thing I hope kept you all reading all those years–the fact that we always tried to do stories we were passionate about, stories that pushed the envelope a bit, that addressed what Batman has meant to us, what he means to us now, what we hope he might mean to our kids. And I *had* stories like that left. Some of the wildest, most daring ones... But if I stayed in Gotham, if I *did* do these stories, I'd need to find a way to do them that'd be different, a way that'd push me as a writer. So how?

And then it came to me. I'd only done Batman with one partner. We'd patrolled Gotham together, always; we'd been a singular team and our stories had focused on the city, on Bruce, Jim Gordon, Alfred... And just as there were villains I still wanted to write out there in the alleys of Gotham, so, too, were there artists–many artists–I was dying to work with on the Caped Crusader. Some were stars, some were up-and-comers. Each was an artist I admired, an artist I knew would push me to reinvent myself and inspire me to reinvent these characters. Tell new stories...

So this idea started to form. What about a series about reinvention, about going places never gone before? If BATMAN had been driving the Batmobile through Gotham, then this series would be taking it off-road, exploring wild new lands. It'd be out of Gotham, a crazy road trip through the outer limits of the mythology, starring the greatest rogues ever assembled. It'd be passionate, about the things that keep us up at night and the things that inspire us right now, today. And above all, it'd be about Batman, because if I learned anything during my run with Greg it's that Batman is about bravery. He's about turning fear into fuel, diving into the scariest unknowns, the mysteries that frighten us. He inspires us to be the heroes we know we can be for ourselves, and for each other.

So a final thank-you before we begin. You all took the ride with me and Greg for five years, and always supported us; the more we pushed into territory that was personal, passionate, the stronger your encouragement became. You taught us–taught me–always to take risks, and create the stories that matter most to us. This series is certainly built in that spirit.

Now hop in, and let's go off-roading :)

SCOTT SNYDER
December 2016

ALL-STAR BATMAN

VOL.1 MY OWN WORST ENEMY

SCOTT SNYDER
writer

JOHN ROMITA JR.
penciller

DANNY MIKI
TOM PALMER * SANDRA HOPE * RICHARD FRIEND
inkers

DEAN WHITE
colorist

DECLAN SHALVEY
artist–"The Cursed Wheel"

JORDIE BELLAIRE
colorist–"The Cursed Wheel"

STEVE WANDS
letterer

JOHN ROMITA JR., DANNY MIKI & DEAN WHITE
collection cover artists

BATMAN created by BOB KANE with BILL FINGER

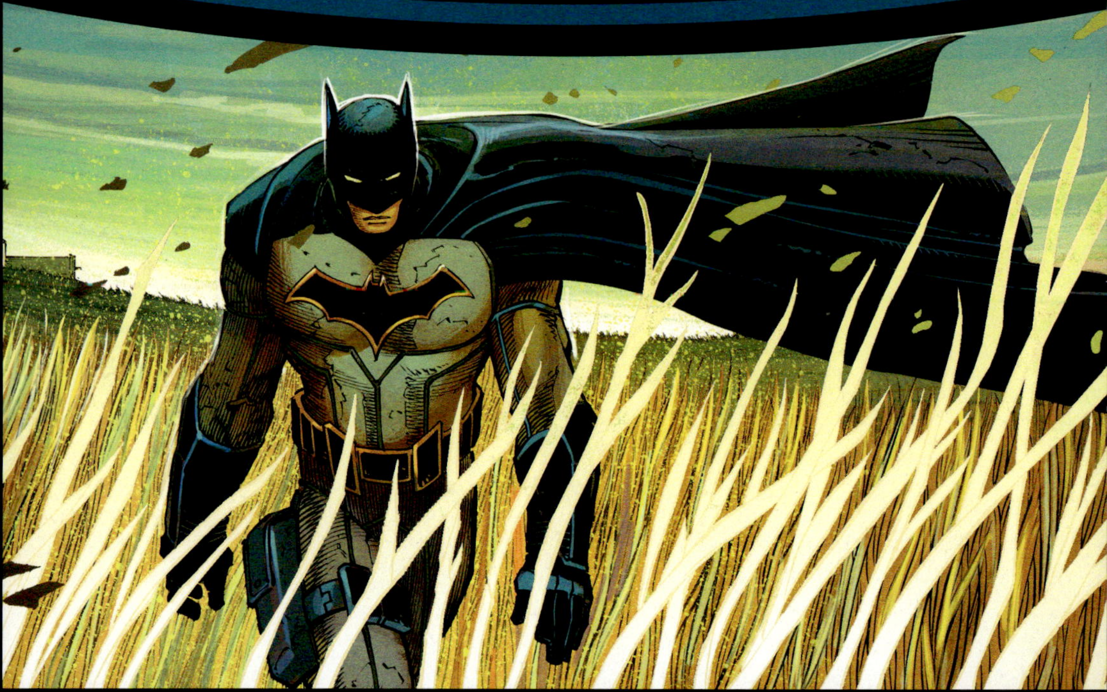

MARK DOYLE Editor - Original Series * **REBECCA TAYLOR** Associate Editor - Original Series * **DAVE WIELGOSZ** Assistant Editor - Original Series
JEB WOODARD Group Editor - Collected Editions * **ROBIN WILDMAN** Editor - Collected Edition * **STEVE COOK** Design Director - Books * **DAMIAN RYLAND** Publication Design

BOB HARRAS Senior VP - Editor-in-Chief, DC Comics

DIANE NELSON President * **DAN DiDIO** Publisher * **JIM LEE** Publisher * **GEOFF JOHNS** President & Chief Creative Officer
AMIT DESAI Executive VP - Business & Marketing Strategy, Direct to Consumer & Global Franchise Management * **SAM ADES** Senior VP - Direct to Consumer
BOBBIE CHASE VP - Talent Development * **MARK CHIARELLO** Senior VP - Art, Design & Collected Editions
JOHN CUNNINGHAM Senior VP - Sales & Trade Marketing * **ANNE DePIES** Senior VP - Business Strategy, Finance & Administration
DON FALLETTI VP - Manufacturing Operations * **LAWRENCE GANEM** VP - Editorial Administration & Talent Relations
ALISON GILL Senior VP - Manufacturing & Operations * **HANK KANALZ** Senior VP - Editorial Strategy & Administration
JAY KOGAN VP - Legal Affairs * **THOMAS LOFTUS** VP - Business Affairs
JACK MAHAN VP - Business Affairs * **NICK J. NAPOLITANO** VP - Manufacturing Administration
EDDIE SCANNELL VP - Consumer Marketing * **COURTNEY SIMMONS** Senior VP - Publicity & Communications
JIM (SKI) SOKOLOWSKI VP - Comic Book Specialty Sales & Trade Marketing * **NANCY SPEARS** VP - Mass, Book, Digital Sales & Trade Marketing

ALL-STAR BATMAN VOL. 1: MY OWN WORST ENEMY

DC Comics, 2900 West Alameda Ave., Burbank, CA 91505. Printed by LSC Communications, Salem, VA, USA. 3/17/17.
First Printing. ISBN: 978-1-4012-6978-4
BARNES & NOBLE VARIANT ISBN: 978-1-4012-7638-6

Library of Congress Cataloging-in-Publication Data is available.

JR JR
16
WHITE

MILES TRAVELED: 0

HEY, CAN'T BLAME THEM FOR HAVING GOOD TASTE.

MACK

STOP. IT'S LIKE END OF TIMES. EVERY FALL IS HOTTER AND THE ***BUGS GET BIGGER.***

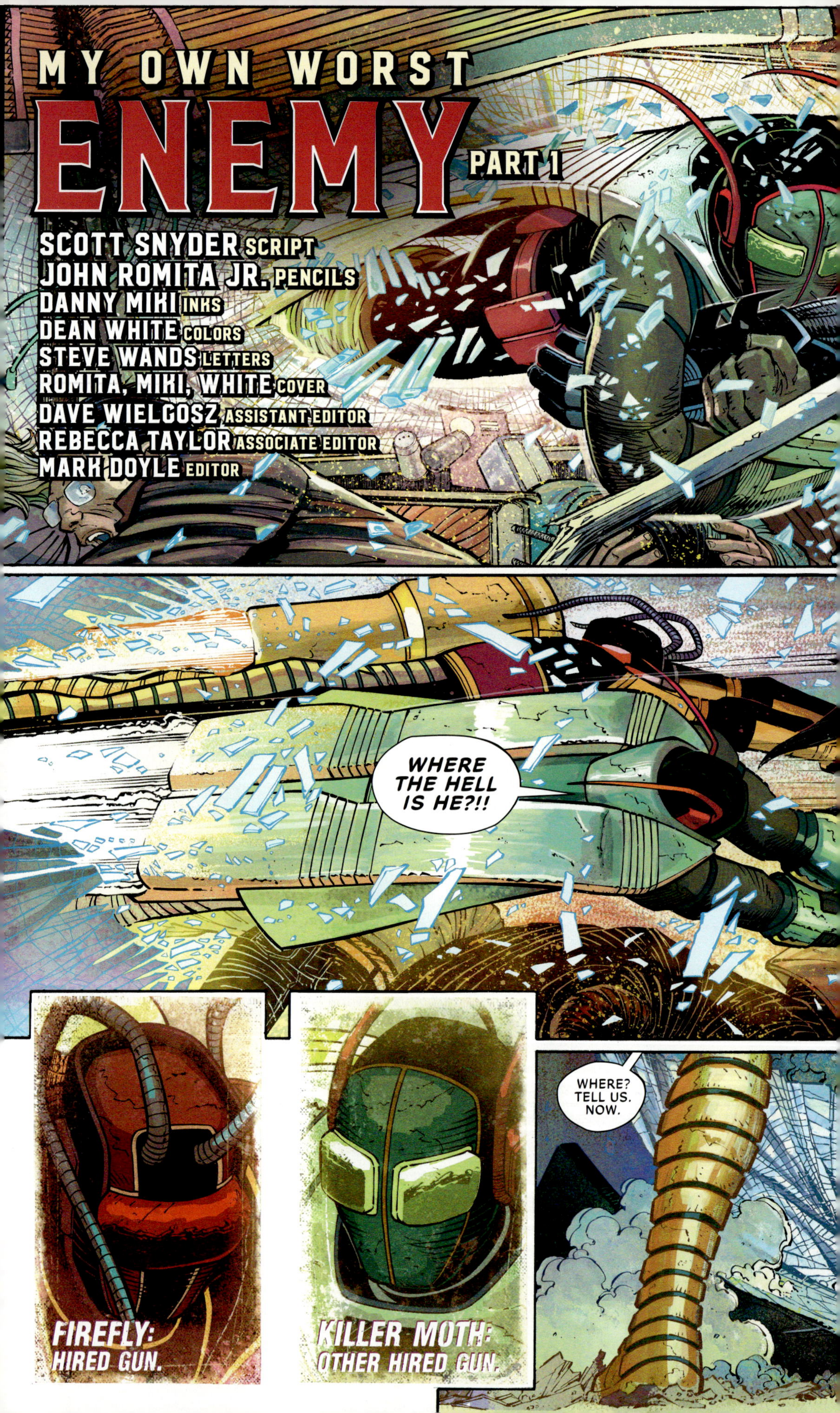
MY OWN WORST
ENEMY PART 1
SCOTT SNYDER SCRIPT
JOHN ROMITA JR. PENCILS
DANNY MIKI INKS
DEAN WHITE COLORS
STEVE WANDS LETTERS
ROMITA, MIKI, WHITE COVER
DAVE WIELGOSZ ASSISTANT EDITOR
REBECCA TAYLOR ASSOCIATE EDITOR
MARK DOYLE EDITOR
WHERE THE HELL IS HE?!!
FIREFLY: HIRED GUN.
KILLER MOTH: OTHER HIRED GUN.
WHERE? TELL US. NOW.

OR EVERYONE IN HERE DIES...

...PAINFULLY.

≷Cough Cough≶
HEY. ALL OF YOU IN THIS DINER. LOOK AT ME. NOT THEM. LOOK AT MY FACE. ***NO ONE IS DYING TODAY.***

WINK

BATMAN:
MOST WANTED
MAN IN THE STATE.

FINE, THEN. THE FIRE WILL EAT...

CLICK

...AND EAT, UNTIL YOU START TALKI--

NG!
WHAT ARE...
THWIP

AAAAGH!
CRUNCH

FINE! THEN THEY DIE BY A MOTH'S ACIDIC--
UNH!
FUN FACT.

MANY ADULT MOTHS HAVE NO MOUTHS AND LIVE LESS THAN A WEEK. I MEAN, REALLY, ONCE THEY REACH MATURITY, THEIR ONLY JOB IS TO SHUT UP AND DIE.

FOOD FOR THOUGHT.
AAIIIIEE!

Huff Huff
COME ON, WE NEED TO GET OUT OF HERE. THERE COULD BE MORE--
SO, IT'S TRUE? WHAT WAS ON THE NEWS? IS HE NEARBY?
DON'T WORRY ABOUT HIM, JUST GET YOURSELF TO S--
IT IS TRUE! YOU BROUGHT HIM HERE! IT'S YOUR FAULT!
SASHA, COME ON NOW, HE SAVED US. HE--
NO! YOU MADE THE WRONG CHOICE, BATMAN! YOU HEAR ME?!
YOU SHOULD NEVER HAVE TAKEN HI OUT OF GOTHAM! YO SHOULD HAVE LET HIM IT'S ALL YOUR FAULT
YOU'RE DRAGGING US ALL--

22 MINUTES AGO.

YOU THREW IT AWAY.

SHUT UP.

SOMEONE WILL FIND IT. SOMEONE *ALWAYS DOES.*

JUST WAIT AND *SEE.*

2 HOURS AGO.
YEAH, WELL, LOOK AT WHAT HE JUST DID TO THE CITY. HE'S A *RATTLESNAKE.* HE LIES LOW UNTIL YOU PULL HIS TAIL. AND THIS...YOU'RE TRYING TO RIP HIS TAIL CLEAN OFF!

FOR GOD'S SAKE, THE WHOLE THING COULD BE A DAMN *TRAP.* YOU EVER THINK OF THAT?!
ONLY EVERY MINUTE SINCE I DECIDED TO DO IT.

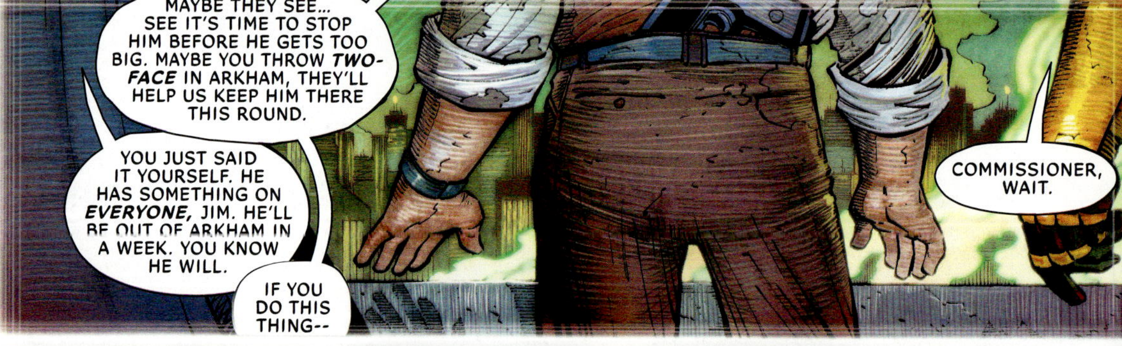
SIGH IT'S JUST...
LOOK, THE CRIME BOSSES HELPED US GET HIM THIS TIME. COBBLEPOT, WHITE, SIONIS.
DON'T.
DENT'S REIGN IS GROWING. HE HAS MORE ON THEM, ON *EVERYONE,* EVERY DAY.
MAYBE THEY SEE... SEE IT'S TIME TO STOP HIM BEFORE HE GETS TOO BIG. MAYBE YOU THROW *TWO-FACE* IN ARKHAM, THEY'LL HELP US KEEP HIM THERE THIS ROUND.
YOU JUST SAID IT YOURSELF. HE HAS SOMETHING ON *EVERYONE,* JIM. HE'LL BE OUT OF ARKHAM IN A WEEK. YOU KNOW HE WILL.
IF YOU DO THIS THING--
COMMISSIONER, WAIT.

THE RAINWATER...IT MIGHT STILL BE *ACIDIC.*

...
THANKS. YOU KNOW, YOU WERE VERY BRAVE. YOU DID GOOD. TRULY.

THANK YOU, BUT...THAT'D BE EASIER TO BELIEVE WITHOUT THE CRIES...

NNNNNGGG...
AHHH!

GHNN!

WELL, YOU DID GOOD EITHER WAY.
SO CAN I CALL YOU *ROBIN?*
I'M TRYING SOMETHING NEW, JIM.

I SHOULD GO.
JUST ANSWER ME THIS. TAKING HIM THERE LIKE THIS. WAS IT *HIS* IDEA...

...OR *YOURS?*

BRUCE...BRUCE...
IF THIS REACHES YOU... YOU HAVE TO KNOW, EVERY TIME HE COMES BACK, IT'S GETTING... **LONGER.** AND HE'S COMING BACK **NOW...**

I'M ALREADY... **LOSING** MYSELF, BRUCE. HE'S GOT TERRIBLE PLANS, TOO. I DON'T KNOW WHAT THEY ARE, BUT I CAN FEEL IT...
LISTEN TO ME, THOUGH. THERE'S **A WAY OUT** THIS TIME. MY PEOPLE, THEY'RE ONLY DAYS AWAY FROM COMPLETING IT... BY THE TIME YOU GET THIS, IT'LL BE READY. YOU NEED TO TAKE ME THERE. YOU KNOW THE **HOUSE** I'M TALKING ABOUT!

2 WEEKS AGO.
*TAKE ME AND **BURN** HIM OUT OF ME ONCE AND FOR ALL.*
DON'T TRY THIS, MASTER BRUCE. PLEASE. FOR ALL WE KNOW, TWO-FACE HAS ***ALREADY*** INFECTED MR. DENT'S MIND. THIS COULD BE A GAME HE'S--

IT WAS ***MY*** IDEA, JIM.

TING

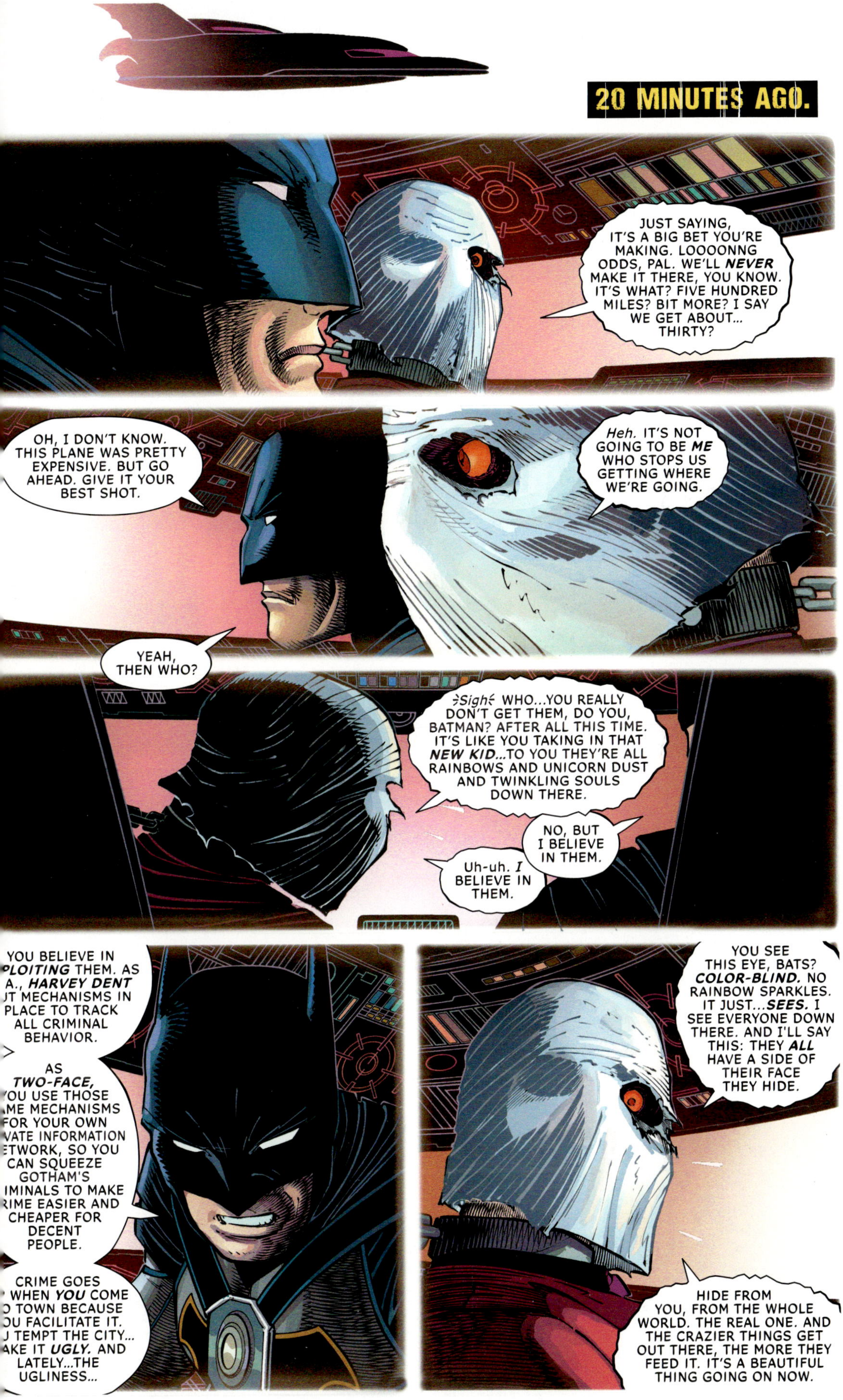

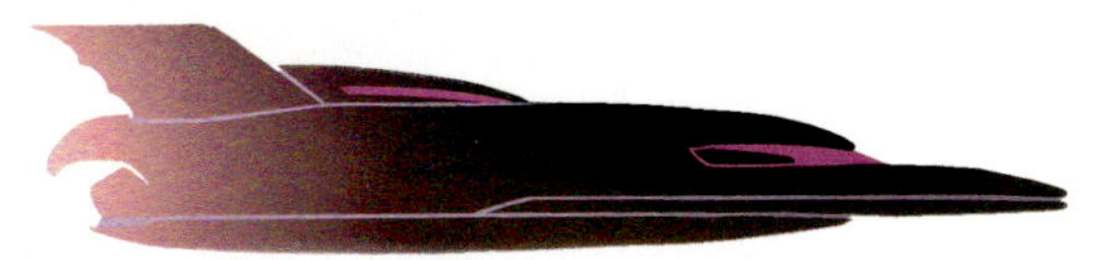

20 MINUTES AGO.

JUST SAYING, IT'S A BIG BET YOU'RE MAKING. LOOOONNG ODDS, PAL. WE'LL ***NEVER*** MAKE IT THERE, YOU KNOW. IT'S WHAT? FIVE HUNDRED MILES? BIT MORE? I SAY WE GET ABOUT... THIRTY?

OH, I DON'T KNOW. THIS PLANE WAS PRETTY EXPENSIVE. BUT GO AHEAD. GIVE IT YOUR BEST SHOT.

Heh. IT'S NOT GOING TO BE ***ME*** WHO STOPS US GETTING WHERE WE'RE GOING.

YEAH, THEN WHO?

Sigh WHO...YOU REALLY DON'T GET THEM, DO YOU, BATMAN? AFTER ALL THIS TIME. IT'S LIKE YOU TAKING IN THAT ***NEW KID***...TO YOU THEY'RE ALL RAINBOWS AND UNICORN DUST AND TWINKLING SOULS DOWN THERE.

NO, BUT I BELIEVE IN THEM.

Uh-uh. *I* BELIEVE IN THEM.

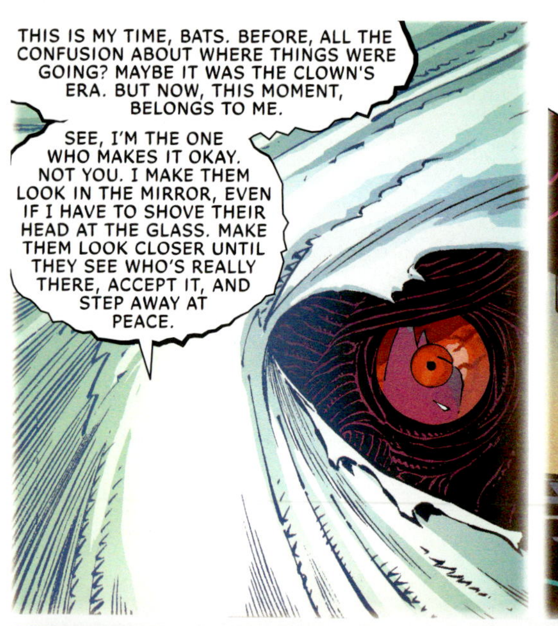
THIS IS MY TIME, BATS. BEFORE, ALL THE CONFUSION ABOUT WHERE THINGS WERE GOING? MAYBE IT WAS THE CLOWN'S ERA. BUT NOW, THIS MOMENT, BELONGS TO ME.
SEE, I'M THE ONE WHO MAKES IT OKAY. NOT YOU. I MAKE THEM LOOK IN THE MIRROR, EVEN IF I HAVE TO SHOVE THEIR HEAD AT THE GLASS. MAKE THEM LOOK CLOSER UNTIL THEY SEE WHO'S REALLY THERE, ACCEPT IT, AND STEP AWAY AT PEACE.

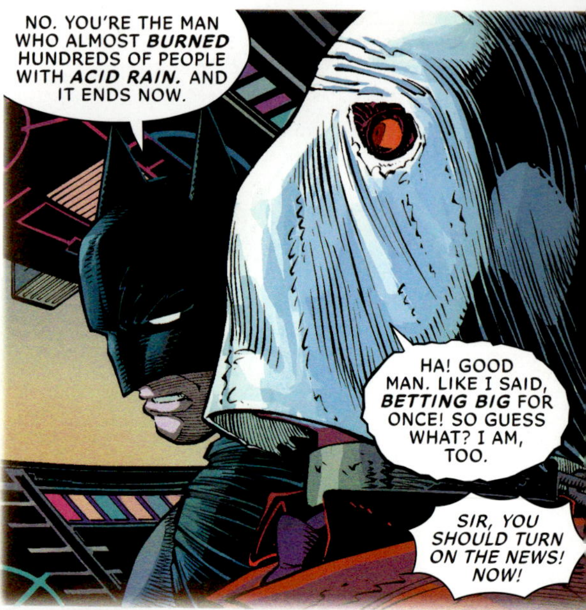
NO. YOU'RE THE MAN WHO ALMOST **BURNED** HUNDREDS OF PEOPLE WITH **ACID RAIN.** AND IT ENDS NOW.
HA! GOOD MAN. LIKE I SAID, **BETTING BIG** FOR ONCE! SO GUESS WHAT? I AM, TOO.
SIR, YOU SHOULD TURN ON THE NEWS! NOW!

TWO FACES DEADLY EAL
NEWS
2 FACE'S EVIL OFFER
AN OFFER U CANT FUSE
WHAT IS IT?
IT'S...AN **OFFER** HE'S MADE.
TO WHO?

TO... ***EVERYONE.***

THAT'S RIGHT, BUDDY. EVERYONE IN GOTHAM, IN THE WHOLE **STATE.** I MADE AN OFFER. I TOLD THEM THAT RIGHT NOW, YOU AND ME, WE'RE FLYING NORTH FROM GOTHAM CITY. AND IF WE GET WHERE WE'RE GOING, EVERYTHING I'VE GOT ON EVERYONE...

...I MEAN **EVERYONE,** IT ALL COMES OUT. EVERY SKELETON. EVERY VISIT TO A BAD PLACE, REAL, ON THE GOOD OL' INTERWEB, THE DARK NET. **EVERYTHING** WILL BE BROUGHT TO LIGHT.

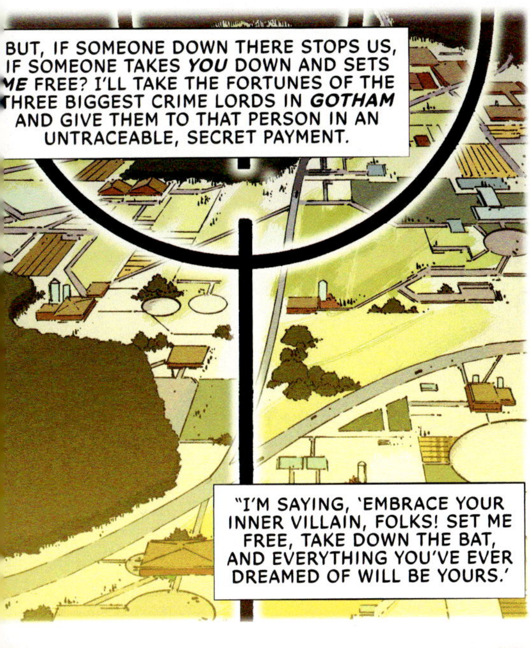
BUT, IF SOMEONE DOWN THERE STOPS US, IF SOMEONE TAKES *YOU* DOWN AND SETS *ME* FREE? I'LL TAKE THE FORTUNES OF THE THREE BIGGEST CRIME LORDS IN *GOTHAM* AND GIVE THEM TO THAT PERSON IN AN UNTRACEABLE, SECRET PAYMENT.
"I'M SAYING, 'EMBRACE YOUR INNER VILLAIN, FOLKS! SET ME FREE, TAKE DOWN THE BAT, AND EVERYTHING YOU'VE EVER DREAMED OF WILL BE YOURS.'

"SO TAKE A LOOK DOWN THERE, BATMAN, AND TELL ME WHAT YOU SEE.
"BECAUSE, ME, I SEE A GAMBLING TABLE. YOU'RE TRYING TO END ME, I'M TRYING TO END YOU. ***ONE LAST HAND.***"

SOMETHING IS HEADED TOWARD YOU!
THAT'S IMPOSSIBLE, WE'RE GHOSTED TO--

SIR, SIR!
SOMEONE MUST KNOW THE CODES! SOMEONE WHO WANTS HIM FREE! CLOSING IN, SIR!

BRACE FOR IMPACT, SIR! BRACE FOR--

RIGHT. NOW.

SCULPTURES
FOR SALE
OR NOT - UP TO YOU
I SAID, ***WHERE IS HE?!*** WE SEARCHED YOUR LITTLE PLANE. WHERE DID YOU HIDE HIM?!

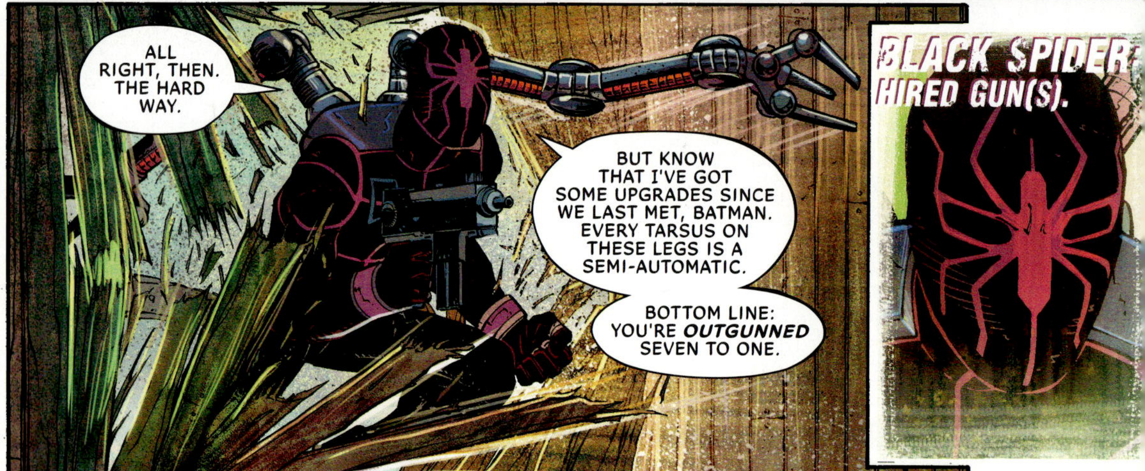
ALL RIGHT, THEN. THE HARD WAY.
BUT KNOW THAT I'VE GOT SOME UPGRADES SINCE WE LAST MET, BATMAN. EVERY TARSUS ON THESE LEGS IS A SEMI-AUTOMATIC.
BOTTOM LINE: YOU'RE ***OUTGUNNED*** SEVEN TO ONE.
BLACK SPIDER:
HIRED GUN(S).

AND IF YOU WON'T TALK, I'LL FIND HIM MYSELF.

BRATTABRATTA

SHK
SHK
SHK
SHK

LIKE I SAID, ***OUTGUNNED.*** NOW IF YOU ONLY HAD THE SENSE TO CARRY INSTEAD OF USING ALL YOUR TRINKETS. I'LL BET YOU'RE REGRETTING IT NOW AREN'T...

...YOU.
WHAT THE--

RPRPBRPRPBP

RPRPBRPRPBP
I'M GOOD.

HUFF HUFF
THERE YOU ARE, YOU...
I'M GONNA...
HUFF HUFF

DAMMIT. WHERE--
HEY.

I JUST WANTED TO SAY...THANKS FOR WHAT YOU DID BACK THERE...

YOU SHOULDN'T BE OUT HERE. HE'S--
I ALSO WANTED TO SAY I'M SORRY.

KLIK

MACK
PUTNAM COUNT
I MEAN THAT. I'M SORRY, BUT YOU...YOU BROUGHT THIS ON YOURSELF NOW HAND HIM OVE

LISTEN TO ME, WHAT HE'S OFFERING, IT'S NOT WORTH WHAT COMES WITH IT. I *PROMISE* YOU...
TING

...THAT.
TING

TING

LOOK WHAT WE HAVE HERE.

NO ONE NEEDS TO GET HURT, BATMAN. JUST LET HIM GO.
NEVER. YOU'RE BETTER THAN THIS. ALL OF YOU.
I SAID LET HIM GO OR... OR--
BLAM

I...DID IT. I DID IT, MR. DENT. THE BATMAN IS--

GOOD JOB. NOW GET THAT THING OUT OF MY FACE.

AND FIND HIS B--

UNH!

WHERE'D HE GO?

WHUMP
UNH!

COUGH COUGH

WHAT ARE YOU--
AGH!

OW!
KLIK
Huff Huff

Heh. REALLY?
BECAUSE EVERYONE OUT THERE? THEY'RE GOING TO GO FOR YOUR HEAD. GOOD GUYS WHO WANT TO BE BAD. BAD GUYS WHO WANT TO BE WORSE.
NOT TO MENTION COBBLEPOT AND CREW, WHO'RE SURE TO SEND A REAL HUNTER AFTER US. THAT'S A WHOLE STATE FULL OF PEOPLE LOOKING TO MAKE YOU ROADKILL, OLD FRIEND.
SO HOW ABOUT YOU JUST TURN AROUND AND TAKE US BACK TO GOTHAM?

I SEE YOUR DAMN BET...
...AND I RAISE.

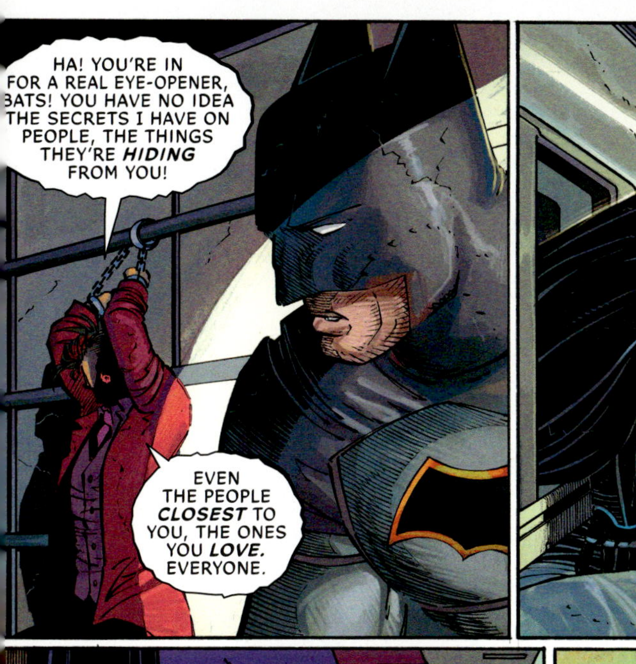
HA! YOU'RE IN FOR A REAL EYE-OPENER, BATS! YOU HAVE NO IDEA THE SECRETS I HAVE ON PEOPLE, THE THINGS THEY'RE *HIDING* FROM YOU!
EVEN THE PEOPLE *CLOSEST* TO YOU, THE ONES YOU *LOVE.* EVERYONE.

TRY NOT TO GET SICK BACK THERE.

PLEASE TELL ME YOU'RE TURNING AROUND, SIR.
I'M PRESSING ON. I'M GETTING HIM TO THAT *HOUSE.* NO MATTER WHAT IT TAKES.

I'M CUTTING OFF COMMUNICATION, ALFRED. TO BRING DOWN THE BATPLANE? SOMEONE *CLOSE* MUST BE WORKING WITH HIM. I NEED TO GO STEALTH ON THIS.
B.F. MOVERS

WAIT, SIR. I NEED TO...I JUST WANT TO SAY--
BATMAN, SIGNING OFF.

I JUST WANT TO SAY...

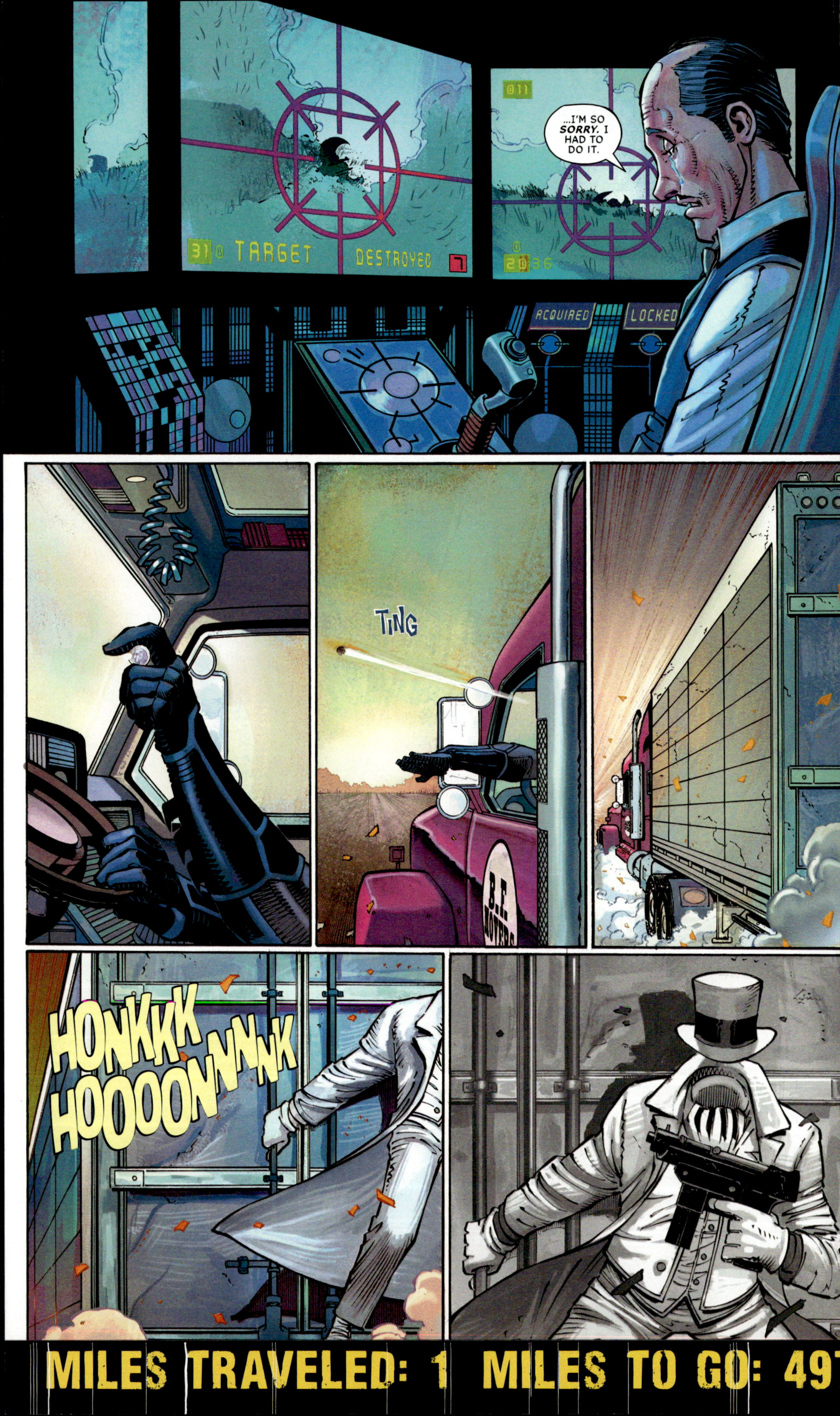

31 TARGET DESTROYED

...I'M SO **SORRY.** I HAD TO DO IT.

ACQUIRED

LOCKED

TING

MILES TRAVELED: 1 MILES TO GO: 49

DAYS FROM NOW.
IT DOESN'T HAVE TO MOVE THIS WAY, YOU KNOW.
WE DON'T HAVE TO KNOCK ON THAT DOOR.
YES. WE DO. I WARNED HIM, HARVEY. TOLD HIM THAT BASTARD HAS TOO MUCH OVER ALL OF US. ME, YOU, THE DEPARTMENT, HIM, THE WHOLE CURSED CITY...
BUT WHAT AM I? A DAMN TREE FALLING IN THE FOREST HE WON'T LOOK AT. IT'S ALL ANY OF US HAVE BEEN. FALLING TREES HE WILLS AWAY.
JIM--
NO. OVER, ARV.
I WANNA GO HOME AND GET A DAMN SHAVE.
NOW COME ON. LET'S DO THIS
JIM GORDON: BATMAN'S CLOSEST ALLY...
...UNTIL TONIGHT.
ALL RIGHT, POLICE, THE CLOCK IS IN THE STUDY. WE TAKE WAYNE MANOR IN THIRTY SECONDS.
DAMN YOU, BRUCE...
WAYNE

"...TONIGHT THE TREE HITS YOU SO HARD, YOU *NEVER* GET BACK UP."
Unh!
MIND GETTING THAT CASH READY, MR. DENT?
IT'S READY, WAYLON. CRIS AND GREEN. CAN YOU SMEL IT? *"BOSS CROC."*
OH, I CAN SMELL IT. ALL THEM LITTLE BILLS.

AYLON JONES:
.A. KILLER CROC.
IMINAL MUSCLE...
VOLVED HUMAN
AIN.

MAKES YOU WEAK, EH, BEING SO FAR FROM YOUR PRECIOUS *GOTHAM?* SEE, ME, I GREW UP IN A SMALL TOWN IN THE EVERGLADES. APPALOOSA. SPENT A LOT OF TIME IN THE *SWAMPS,* ALONE. WRESTLING ALLIGATORS, SNAKES...

...EVERYONE THOUGHT I WAS SOME KIND OF *TOWN FOOL.* BUT I WAS LEARNING TO SURVIVE OUTSIDE MY COMFORT ZONE. BE VICIOUS...

YOU, I EXPECTED MORE FROM YOU. ***HELL, I EVEN BROUGHT MY OWN MUSCLE...***

TRIXIE:
A.K.A. KING SHARK. BIGGER CRIMINAL MUSCLE...EVOLVED SHARK BRAIN.

Y OWN WORST ENEMY PART 2

OTT SNYDER SCRIPT
HN ROMITA JR. PENCILS
NNY MIKI INKS
AN WHITE COLORS
EVE WANDS LETTERS
MITA, MIKI, WHITE COVER
VE WIELGOSZ ASSISTANT EDITOR
BECCA TAYLOR ASSOCIATE EDITOR
RK DOYLE EDITOR

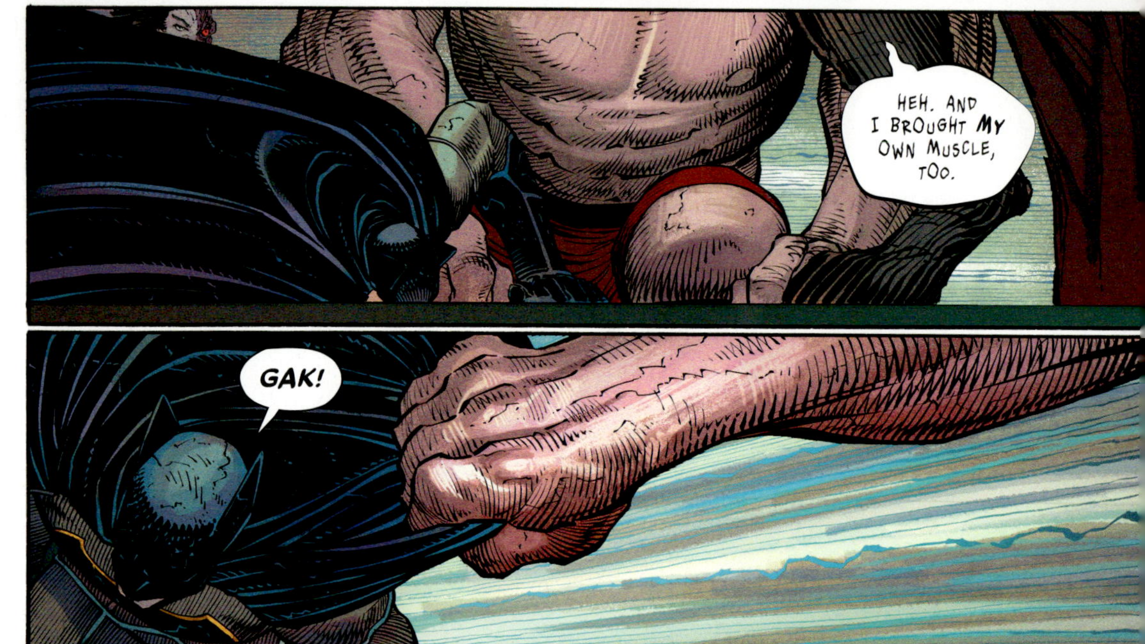
HEH. AND I BROUGHT MY OWN MUSCLE, TOO.
GAK!

YOU TALL, BATMAN.

AARON HELZINGER: A.K.A. AMYGDALA: BIGGEST CRIMINAL MUSCLE...
...PARTIAL BRAIN.
I FIX TALL.

AAWHOOOOOOOOOOOOOooo--
HEAR THAT, BATS?!
THAT'S THE SOUND OF RECKONING, PAL! GROWING LOUDER AND LOUDER IN YOUR EARS UNTIL YOU CAN'T BLOCK IT OUT ANYM--
KLIK KLIK
KLIK KLIK
oooooooooooo
SORRY. WERE YOU SAYING SOMETHING, DENT? I MUST HAVE MISSED IT.

POOM
POOOM
TOO CROWDED ON THIS CAR TO HEAR MUCH.
UNH! THAT SMELL...
AAAAAHHH! GET IT OFF!
Oof!
HEH. WHAT WERE THOSE THINGS? SHARK REPELLENT? SMELLS LIKE--
DEAD SHARK MATTER? COPPER ACETATE MIXED WITH BORIC ACID. COME HERE. I'LL LET YOU TASTE CROC ROT.
AW, SEE, I'M THICKER-SKINNED THAN MY FRIENDS, HOSS. SO TOSS YOUR LITTLE SCENTED BATARANGS AND TAKE YOUR BESSSS...
...SSSST...

TING
TING
SSSSSSHHHHH...
...OT.
THUNK
OW.
HEY, WAYLON. APPALOOSA CALLED...
...THEY WANT THEIR *FOOL* BACK.

MILES TRAVELED: 156 MILES TO GO: 34

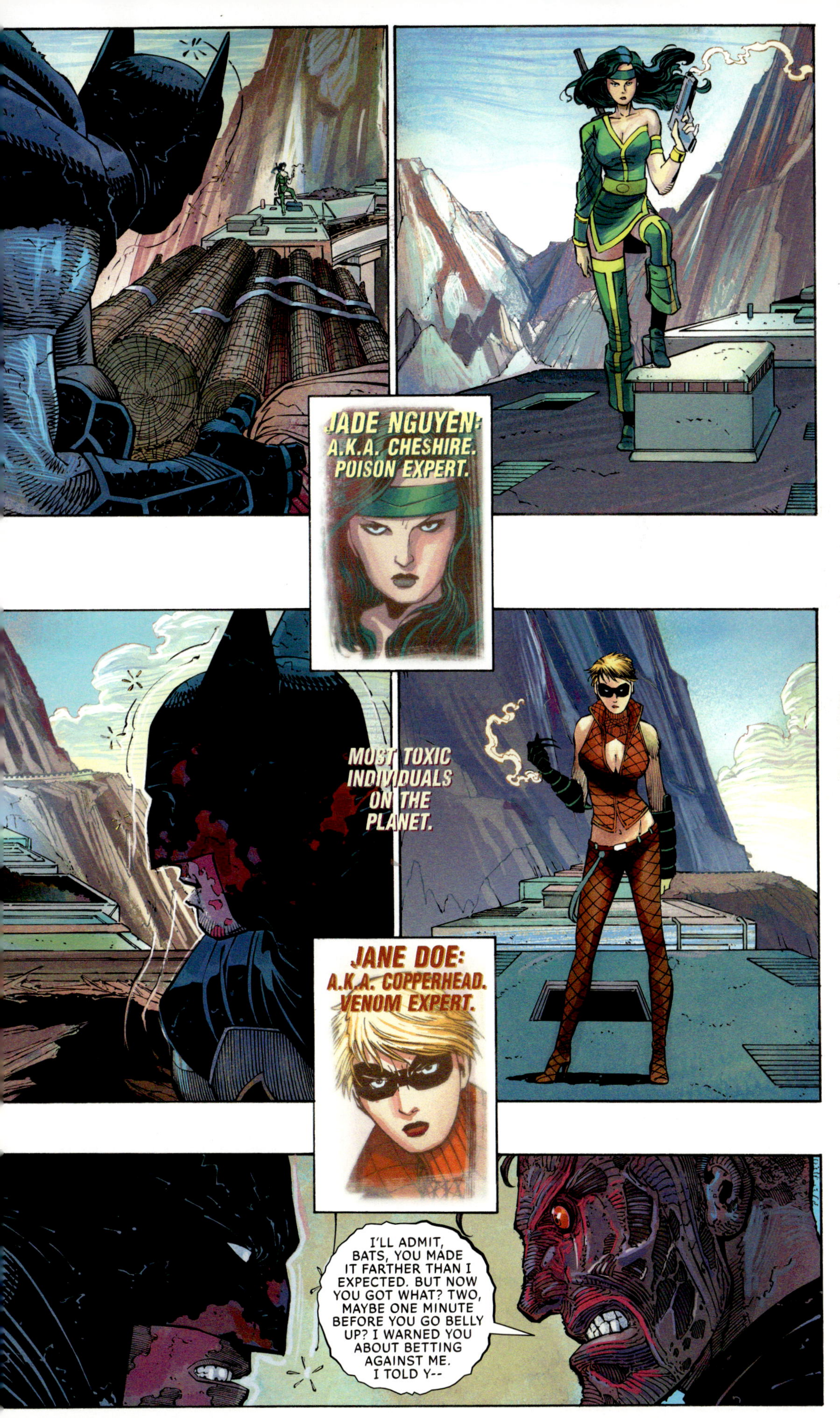
JADE NGUYEN:
A.K.A. CHESHIRE.
POISON EXPERT.
MOST TOXIC INDIVIDUALS ON THE PLANET.
JANE DOE:
A.K.A. COPPERHEAD.
VENOM EXPERT.
I'LL ADMIT, BATS, YOU MADE IT FARTHER THAN I EXPECTED. BUT NOW YOU GOT WHAT? TWO, MAYBE ONE MINUTE BEFORE YOU GO BELLY UP? I WARNED YOU ABOUT BETTING AGAINST ME. I TOLD Y--

THUK
GAK!
Huh. LOOK AT THAT. NOW YOU HAVE ONE MINUTE TO LIVE, TOO. AND I'M THE ONLY ONE WHO CAN MAKE AN ANTIDOTE.
COUGH AND WITH THAT DESPERATE LITTLE PARLOR TRICK, YOU BOUGHT YOURSELF WHAT, A FEW MORE @$#! MILES?
I'LL !#@$ TAKE THEM.
WAIT, WHAT THE HELL ARE YOU...
I THREW MY CHARGES THE SECOND I SAW CROC. GET READY.
THIS IS OUR STOP.
YOU CAN'T BE--
KLIK
BOOOM
BOOOM

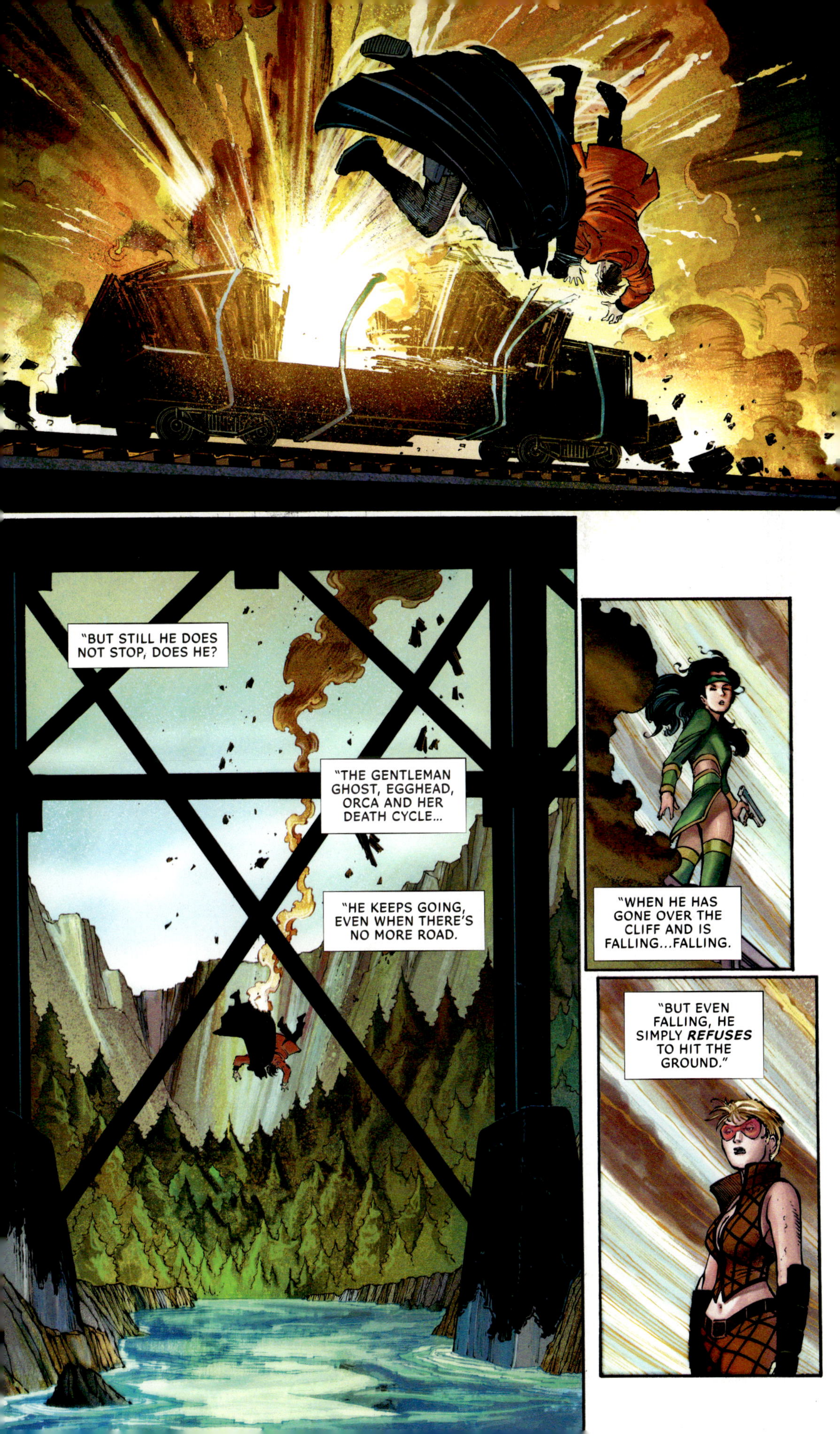

"BUT STILL HE DOES NOT STOP, DOES HE?

"THE GENTLEMAN GHOST, EGGHEAD, ORCA AND HER DEATH CYCLE...

"HE KEEPS GOING, EVEN WHEN THERE'S NO MORE ROAD.

WHICH IS WHY YOU HAVE COME TO ME.
IS IT NOT?

20 HOURS AGO.
SIX STORIES BELOW THE NOW-CLOSED, HISTORIC RUSSIAN TEA ROOM.

HERE, MR. KNYAZEV. WE COME BEARING GIFTS.
VODKA, BUT IT'S AMERICAN. NOT RUSSIAN. THE VERY FINEST.

WARREN WHITE: A.K.A. GREAT WHITE.
ROMAN SION
A.K.A. BLACK MA
OSWALD COBBLEPOT: A.K.A. PENGUIN
GOTHAM'S LORDS OF ORGANIZED CRIME A.K.A. THE BLACK AND WHITES.

I MUST SAY, IT'S SOMETHING TO LAY EYES ON YOU. WE ALL THOUGHT YOU WERE...

...RETIRED.

BY RETIRED HE MEANS %^&*@$ DEAD.
SO WHAT THEY SAY IS TRUE THEN, Eh?

AND WHAT DO THEY SAY?
KLIK

DO TELL.

NOTHING. I JUST MEANT--

WHAT MY ASSOCIATE MEANT WAS THAT BIRDS ON THE STREET, THEY SPEAK OF YOU AS A GREAT LEGEND. THEY SAY THAT WHEN THE SOVIET UNION COLLAPSED, THE ***U.S. GOVERNMENT*** ACQUIRED YOU FOR ITSELF AND--

"ACQUIRED" ME?

APOLOGIES. I MEANT... ***OFFERED YOU A JOB*** KILLING FOR THEM. THEY ENHANCED YOU ALL OVER AGAIN, IN ***NEW*** WAYS... ***STRONGER*** WAYS. BIRDS, THEY SAY OVER THE PAST DECADE YOU'VE KILLED MORE HOSTILES THAN ANYONE ALIVE.
THEY SAY YOU'RE THE RICHEST, DEADLIEST CONTRACT KILLER IN THE STATES.
BIRDS ON THE STREET ARE DIRTY, ***DISEASED*** THINGS.

TOGETHER, AS A TEAM, WE'VE GOT JUST ENOUGH TO PAY YOUR FEE.
DAMN IF IT AIN'T AN ECONOMY IN ITS--
ENOUGH, WARREN. ANATOLI...PLEASE. I KNOW YOU'RE EXCLUSIVE TO D.C.
SIGH BATMAN...
I HAVE BEEN WAITING A LONG TIME FOR YOU ALL TO BECOME MEN AND HIRE ME TO KILL HIM.
I WILL DO THIS FOR YOU, ON ONE CONDITION.
ANYTHIN
EVERY JOB I EVER DO, MY WHOLE LIFE, IT NEEDS TO BE QUIET. BUT NOW...NOW I HAVE ALMOST EVERYTHING I NEED TO MAKE MY OWN DREAM, MY ***SECRET*** DREAM SINCE BOYHOOD, CONCRETE. SO FOR THIS JOB, FOR BATMAN, I FINALLY GET TO BE ***LOUD.*** YOU CLEAN UP THE MESS.
...***MESS?*** WHAT KIND OF--
YES, OF COURSE. WHATEVER THE TERMS, WE'RE IN.
GOOD.
THERE ***WILL*** BE MESS.

IT'S ALL MINE NOW, SEE?! YER ONEY. YER JEWELS. 'ERYTHING AT THIS DOUBLE FEATURE BELONGS TO TWO-FACE!
SEE. THERE. IGHT THERE. THAT'S THE TWO-FACE I KNOW. NOT...
...THAT.
SO WHAT HAPPENED? WAS IT THE GUNSHOT HE--?
NO, IT'S JUST HIM, MASTER DUKE.

ALSO 20 HOURS AGO.
WHEN YOU'RE YOUNG, THAT'S HOW YOU KNOW TWO-FACE. FOR HIS LOUDER EXPLOITS.
BUT THE KEY TO UNDERSTANDING HIM IS THAT HE'S TWO MINDS TRAPPED IN ONE BODY. WHEN HE'S HARVEY, HE'S A TRULY GOOD SOUL. WHEN HE'S TWO-FACE, HE REVELS IN HUMAN DARKNESS. THE CHANGE HOLDS FOR MONTHS AT A TIME.

WHAT HARVEY KNOWS, TWO-FACE DOES NOT. WHAT TWO-FACE KNOWS, HE KEEPS HIDDEN FROM HARVEY.
AS FOR THE TWO-FACE CHILDREN KNOW, MASTER BRUCE HAS A THEORY...WHEN THE CHANGE IS ABOUT O OCCUR AND MR. DENT S RETURNING TO THEIR SHARED MIND, HE CAUSES TWO-FACE TO ACT OUT, SO HE'LL BE CAUGHT.
HENCE THE DIFFERENCE BETWEEN THE TWO-FACE IN THE UITS AND SUCH, AND THE ONE PARENTS KNOW ALL TOO WELL--THE SECRET, DARKER MAN WHO MAKES EVIL...EASY.
WAIT. ANY MEMORIES FROM BEFORE THE ACID ATTACK ARE STILL SHARED, RIGHT? WHICH MEANS THAT TWO-FACE MUST KNOW THAT BATMAN IS--
YES. STILL, IN THIS CITY, GUESSING BRUCE WAYNE IS BATMAN ISN'T THAT DIFFICULT. IT'S PROVING THE LINK THAT MASTER BRUCE HAS MADE IMPOSSIBLE.
I LOOK AT THE MAP AND I JUST HOPE TO GOD TWO-FACE DOESN'T HAVE CLAWS IN SOMEONE CLOSE ENOUGH TO MASTER BRUCE TO PROVIDE THE LINK.

MAN, ALL THIS FOR SOME POSSIBLE CURE FOR TWO-FACE. CAN YOU PULL UP WHAT WE HAVE, ALFRED?
MR. DENT HAS BEEN FUNDING IT HIMSELF. THE LAST VERSION HE SENT MASTER BRUCE IS THIS.
...WAIT, THAT?
IS THAT CHEMICAL...
...OH NO.
WHAT IS IT, MASTER DUKE?

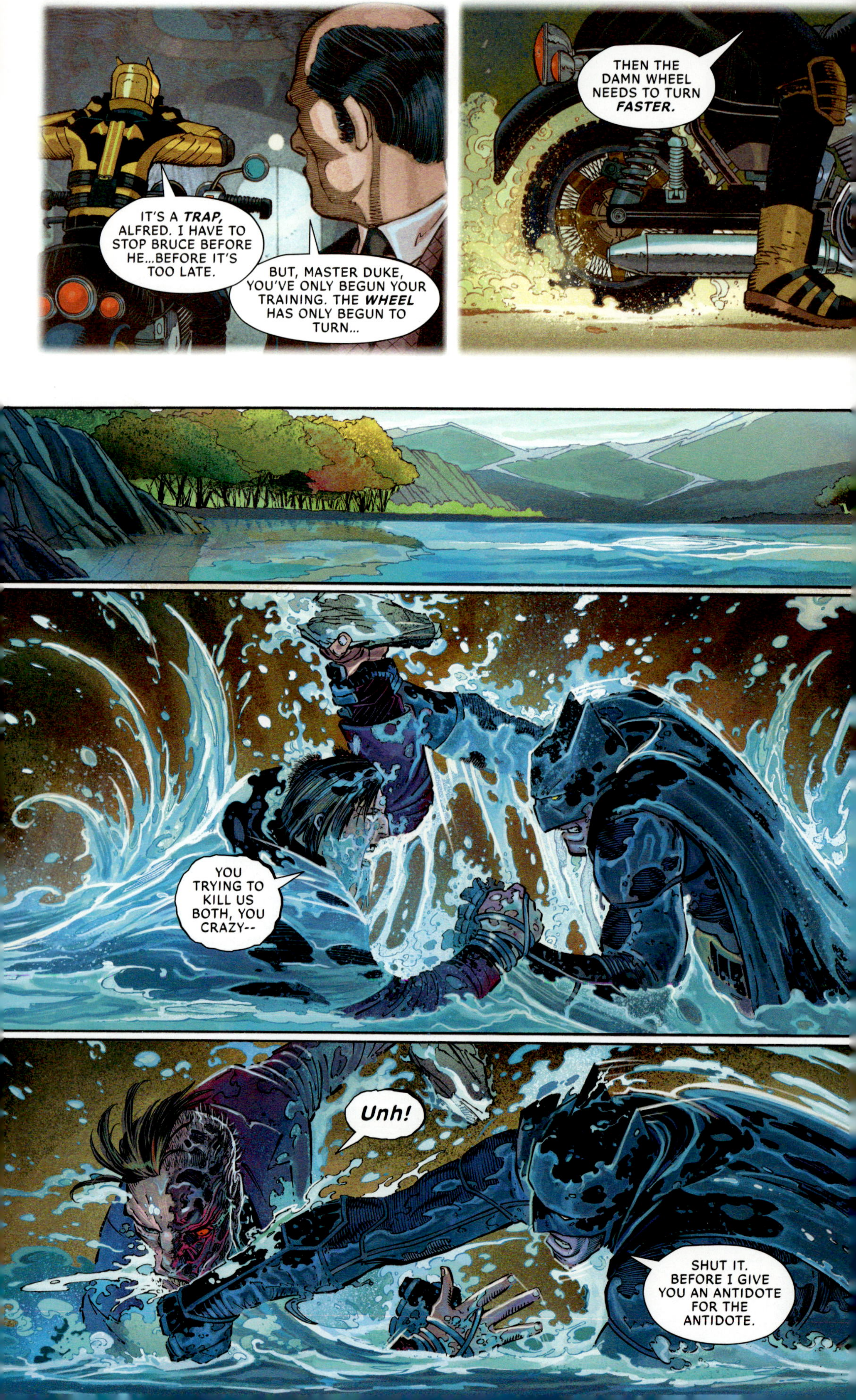

YOU TRYING TO KILL US BOTH, YOU CRAZY--

⸗COUGH⸗ Heh. LET ME ASK YOU SOMETHING, BOSS. YOU GET ME WHERE WE'RE GOING, ALL THEIR SECRETS COME OUT--YOU THINK YOU'LL BE THEIR SAVIOR? YOU THINK THEY'LL *THANK* YOU?

IN THE END.
GET UP.

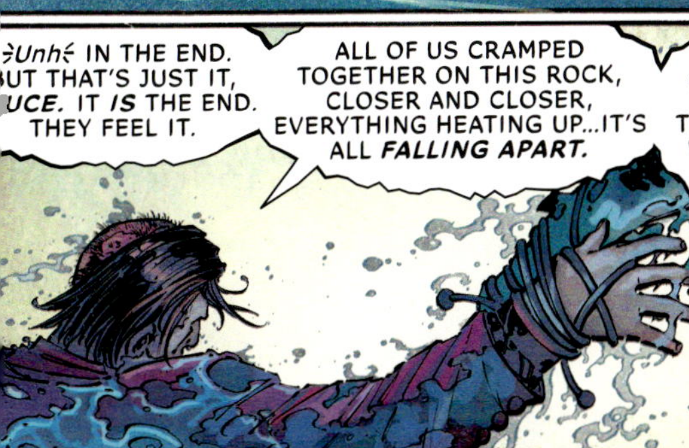
⸗Unh⸗ IN THE END. UT THAT'S JUST IT, UCE. IT *IS* THE END. THEY FEEL IT.
ALL OF US CRAMPED TOGETHER ON THIS ROCK, CLOSER AND CLOSER, EVERYTHING HEATING UP...IT'S ALL *FALLING APART.*
THEY'RE TIRED OF ACTING LIKE THEY OUGHT TO BE IN PUBLIC, RATHER THAN WHO THEY *ARE*...THEY WANT TO BE THEMSELVES. TO BE BAD. STOP TRYING TO DRAG--

WALK. THE ROAD IS JUST AHEAD.
YOU AND HARVEY, THOUGH, YOU ACTUALLY BELIEVE THEY ALL *WANT* TO GET CAUGHT, GO BEFORE THE GREAT JUDGE, CRY IT OUT, BE *REDEEMED.*

I WONDER IF THAT'S HOW IT'D BE FOR YOU. IF I COULD FINALLY JOIN YOUR TWO HALVES? IF I HAD THE PROOF?
WHEN THAT DAY COMES, I STAND BY WHAT I'VE DONE. I'M READY.

Huh. FUNNY YOU SHOULD SAY THAT.

WHAT--

BLAMM

HARV.
BRUCE. YOU CAME.

OF COURSE I DID.
NO, I MEAN IT. THANK YOU FOR BELIEVING IN...THIS.
IT'S SOMETH SPECIA
IT WILL BE. I HOPE.

HEY. YOU DROPPED THIS.

MY COIN?
BRUCE, BUT HOW DID YOU...

"IT ALWAYS COMES BACK..."

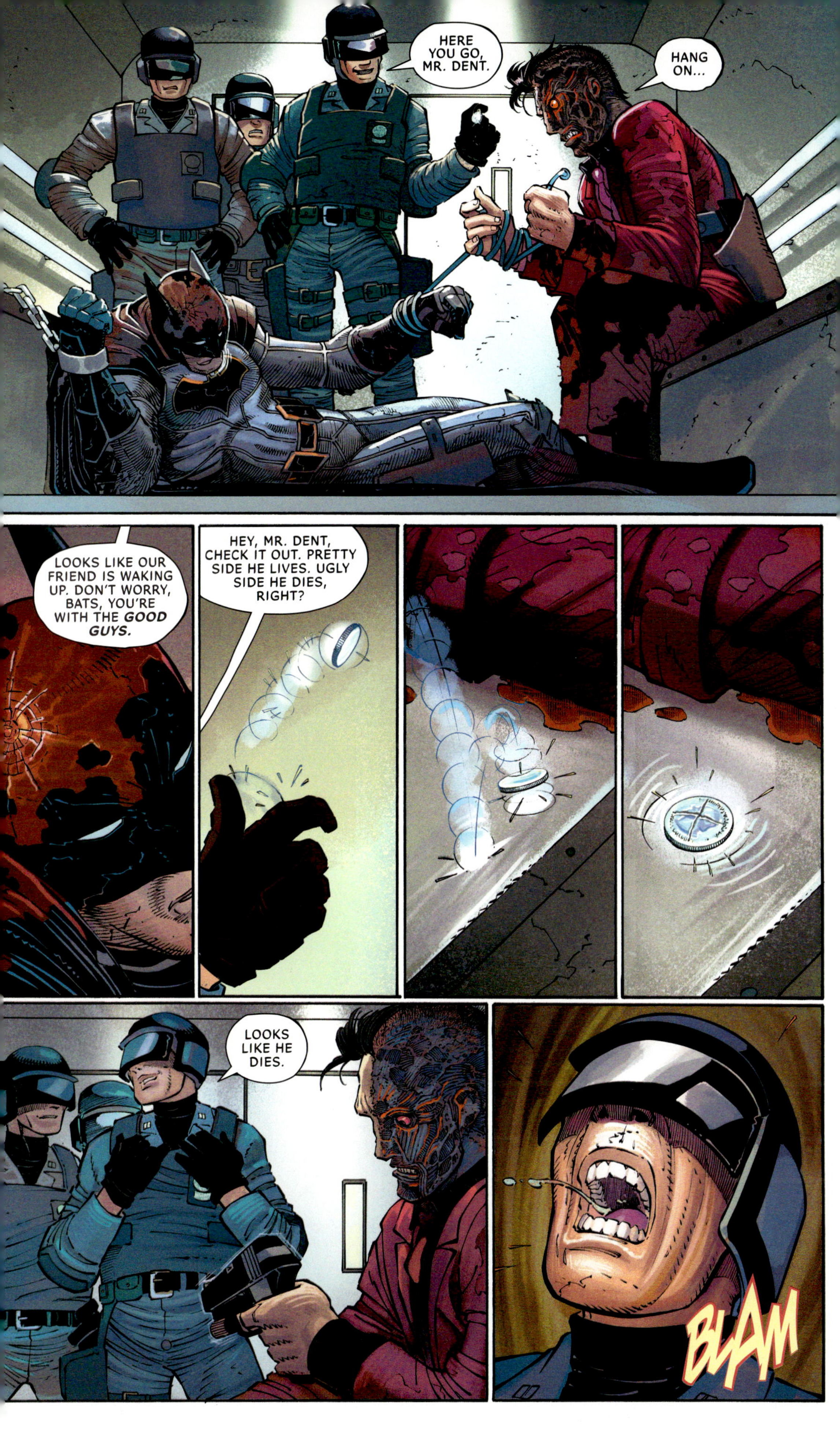

HERE YOU GO, MR. DENT.

HANG ON...

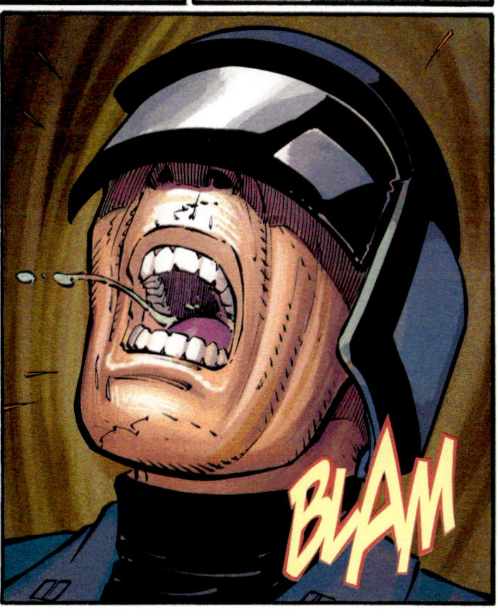

IS THAT
HOW MY COIN
WORKS?

ALL RIGHT, BATS. BELIEVE ME, ONE THING I NEVER DO IS LIE, AND THIS WAY, YOU'RE GETTING OFF EASY.

SEE, RIGHT NOW THE PROOF ABOUT YOU? IT'S ON THE MAYOR'S DESK. YOU'D KEPT COMING? IT'D DE-ENCRYPT. BUT IF YOU'D ***STILL*** KEPT COMING? WHAT I WOULD HAVE SHOWN YOU? KILLING YOU NOW IS ***MERCY STREET.***

BECAUSE WHEN IT COMES TO SECRETS? TO HUMAN EVIL? THERE'S ALWAYS ***SOMETHING WORSE*** DOWN THE ROAD.

I CAN'T WAIT.
AGH!
KRACK

WHAT THE HELL'S GOING ON BACK THERE? SOUNDS LIKE--
HOLD ON. LOOK UP AHEAD...

WHAT...IN GOD'S NAME IS THAT?

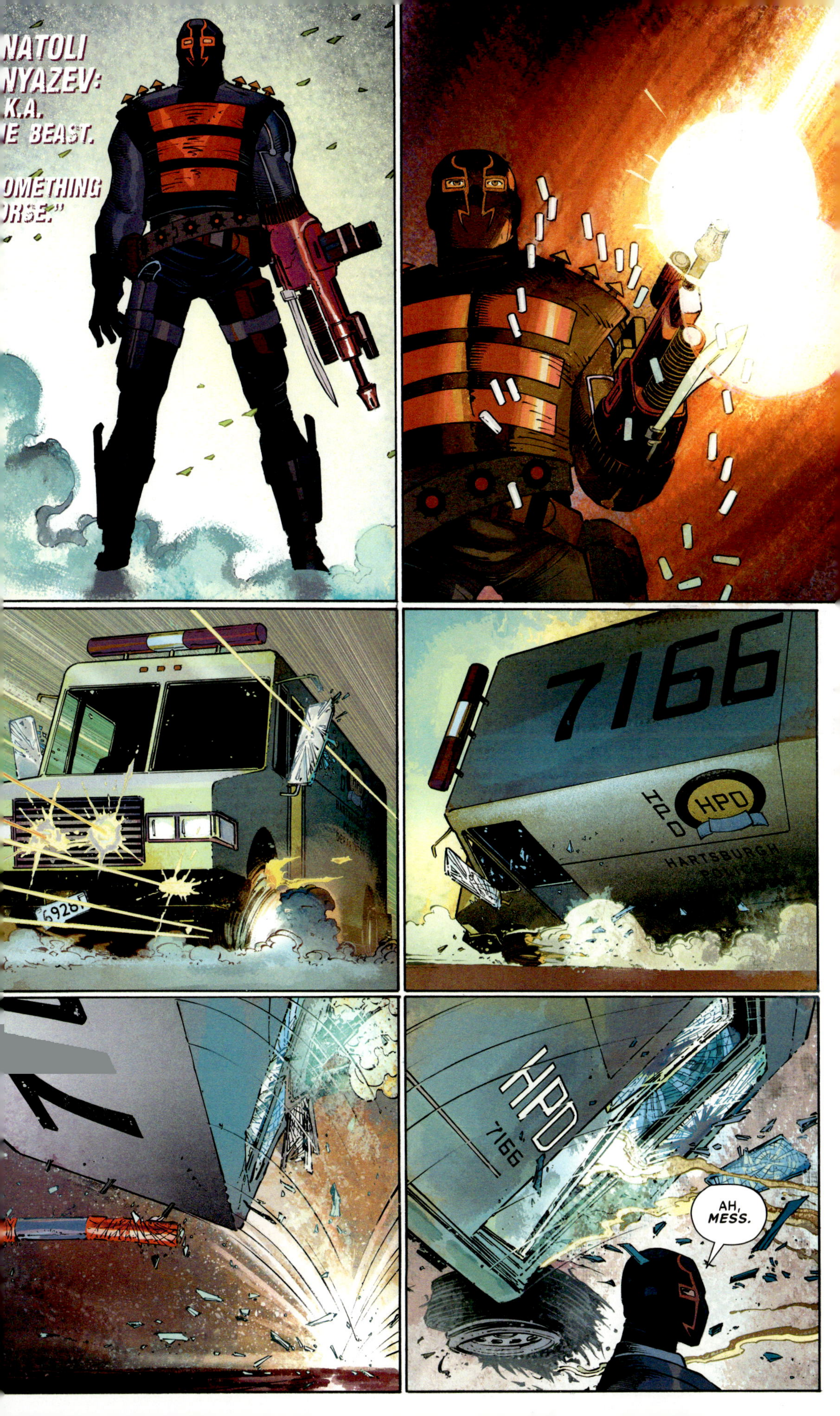

NATOLI
NYAZEV:
K.A.
E BEAST.

OMETHING
RSE."

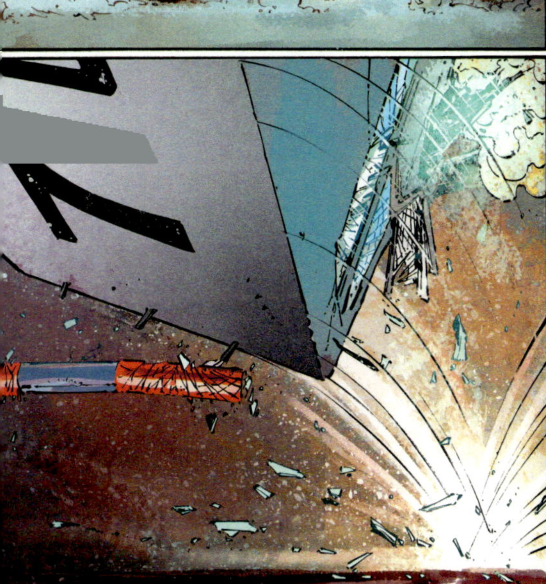

MILES TRAVELED: 171 MILES TO GO: 327

AND 2 DAYS FROM NOW.

I CAN AND I WILL, MR. PENNYWORTH. YOU AND I KNOW I HAVE NO CHOICE. HE BROUGHT THIS ON HIMSELF.

I SAID OUT OF THE WAY. NOW. HARVEY, OPEN IT.

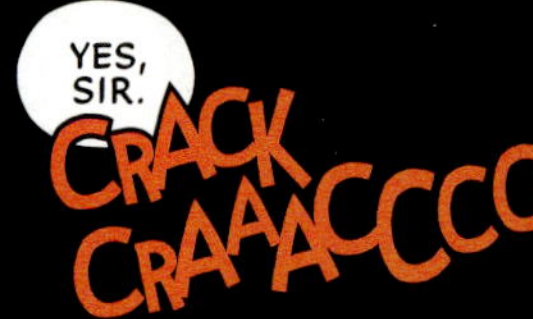

JRJR
16
White

JRJR
16
White

THEN.
THERE'S AN INVENTION COMING THAT'S GOING TO CHANGE THE WAY WE LIVE. I'M TELLING YOU.
SURE THERE IS.
I HEARD ABOUT IT. IT'S A COMPUTER, BUT IT'S A CONTACT LENS YOU WEAR ON YOUR EYE.
YOU CAN PULL UP WHATEVER INFORMATION YOU WANT, SURE, BUT YOU CAN ALSO SKIN THE WORLD HOWEVER YOU WANT TO SEE IT, YOU KNOW?
NOPE.
SIGH I MEAN, YOU WANT TO SEE THE SKY FULL OF DRAGONS, YOU CAN. YOU WANT TO SEE YOUR DAD LOOK LIKE A KNIGHT, YOU CAN.
YOU SEE IT YOUR WAY AND NO ONE KNOWS. UNLESS YOU TELL THEM. SO HERE, YOU TELL ME WHAT YOU'D SEE, AND I'LL TELL YOU WHAT I'D SEE.
RIGHT NOW? I'M RELAXING.
MY OWN WORST ENEMY PART 3
SCOTT SNYDER SCRIPT
JOHN ROMITA JR. PENCILS
DANNY MIKI INKS
DEAN WHITE COLORS
STEVE WANDS LETTERS
ROMITA, MIKI, WHITE COVER
DAVE WIELGOSZ ASSISTANT EDITOR
REBECCA TAYLOR ASSOCIATE EDITOR
MARK DOYLE EDITOR
NOW.
GO ON. LOOK THROUGH YOUR LENS, AND TELL ME WHAT YOU SEE OUT THERE.

NOW.
MILES TRAVELED: 171 MILES TO GO: 327

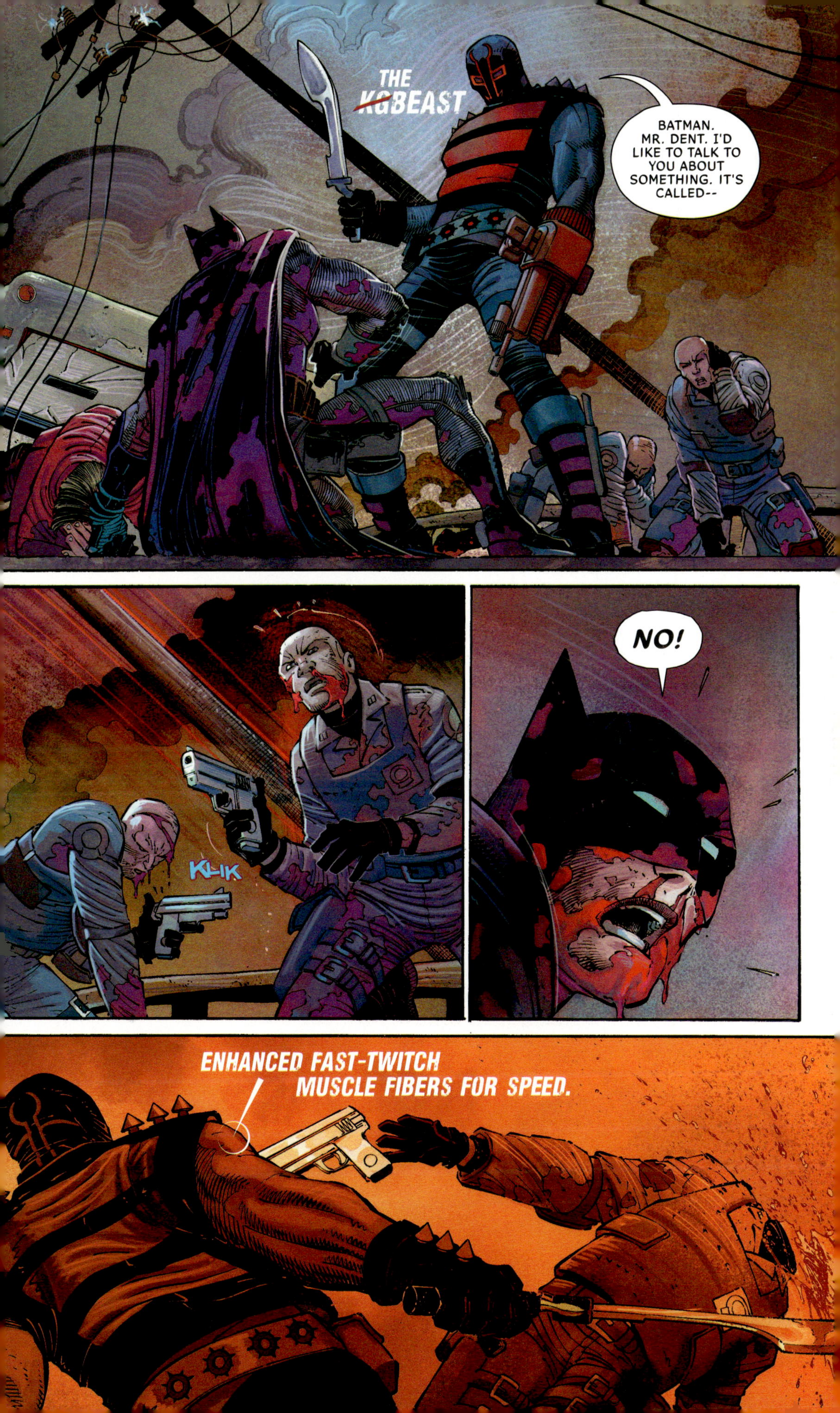

THE KGBEAST

BATMAN. MR. DENT. I'D LIKE TO TALK TO YOU ABOUT SOMETHING. IT'S CALLED--

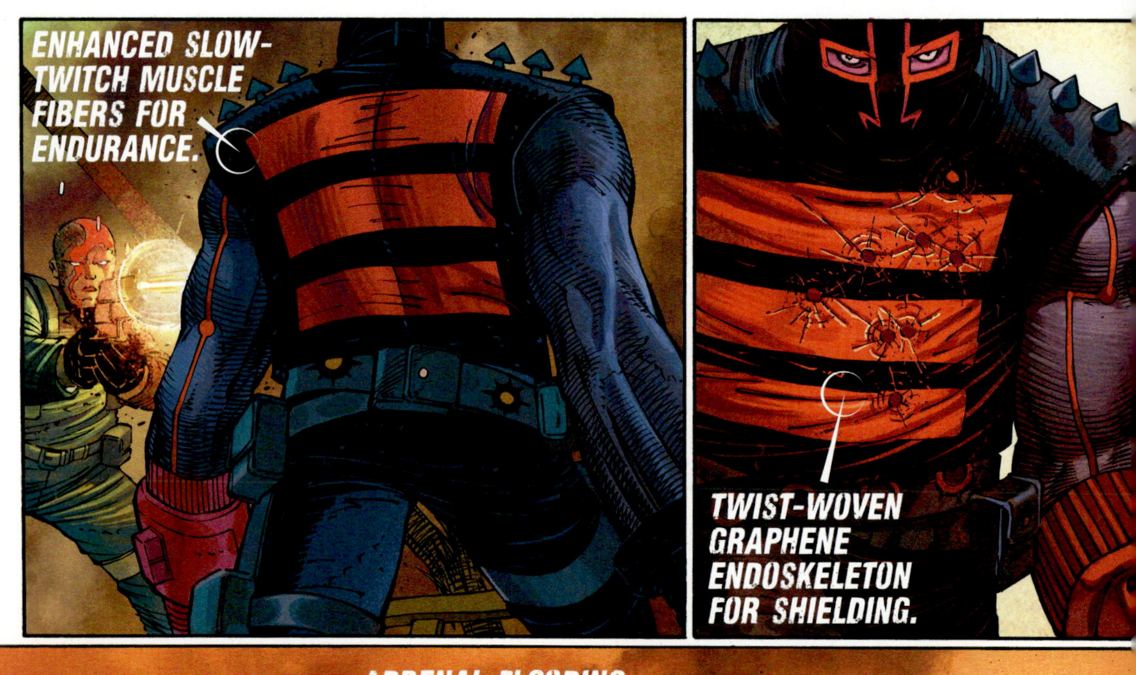
ENHANCED SLOW-TWITCH MUSCLE FIBERS FOR ENDURANCE.
TWIST-WOVEN GRAPHENE ENDOSKELETON FOR SHIELDING.

ADRENAL FLOODING FOR "HYSTERICAL STRENGTH."

PROSTHETIC COMBINATION BROWNING M2HB HEAVY MACHINE GUN. M203 GRENADE LAUNCHER
(AND SELF-SHARPENING MACHETE).

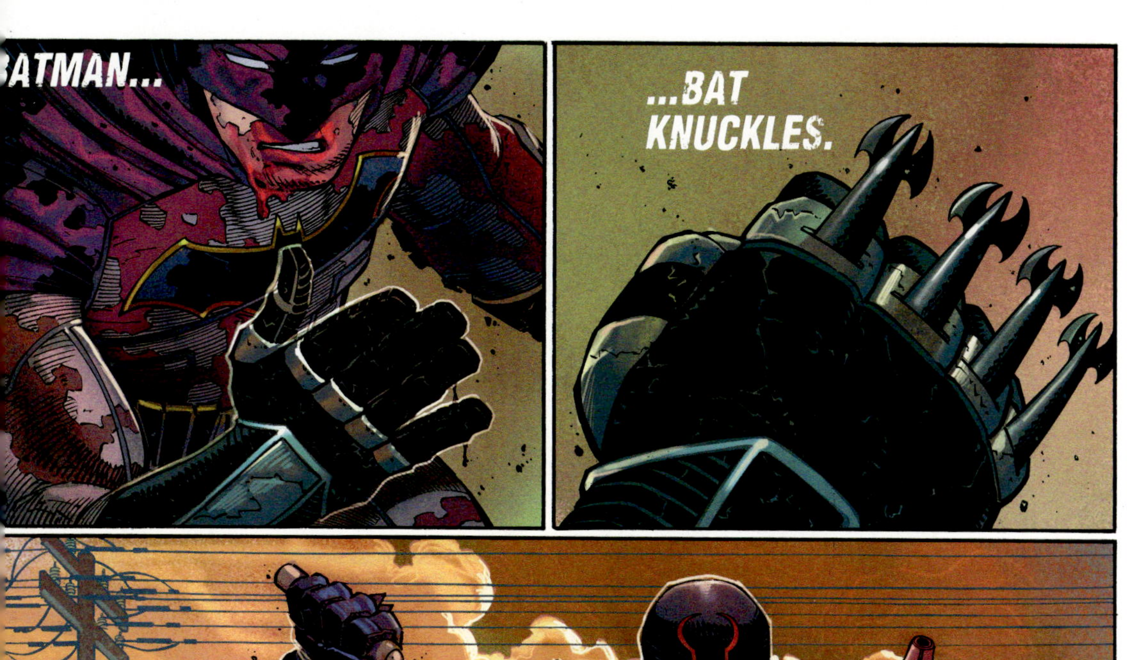
BATMAN...
...BAT
KNUCKLES.

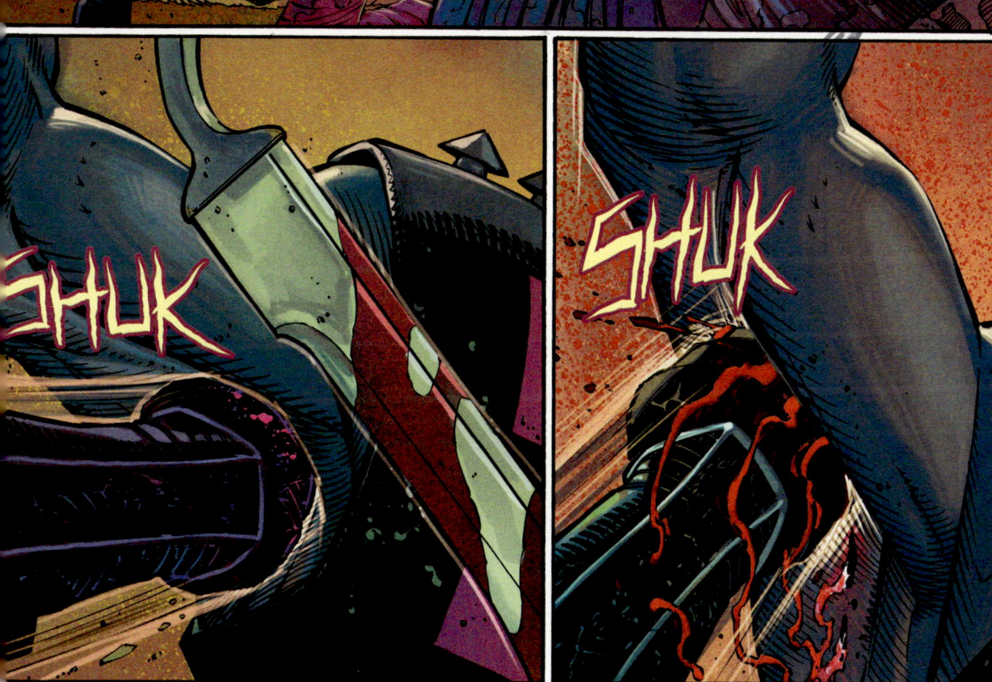
SHUK
SHUK

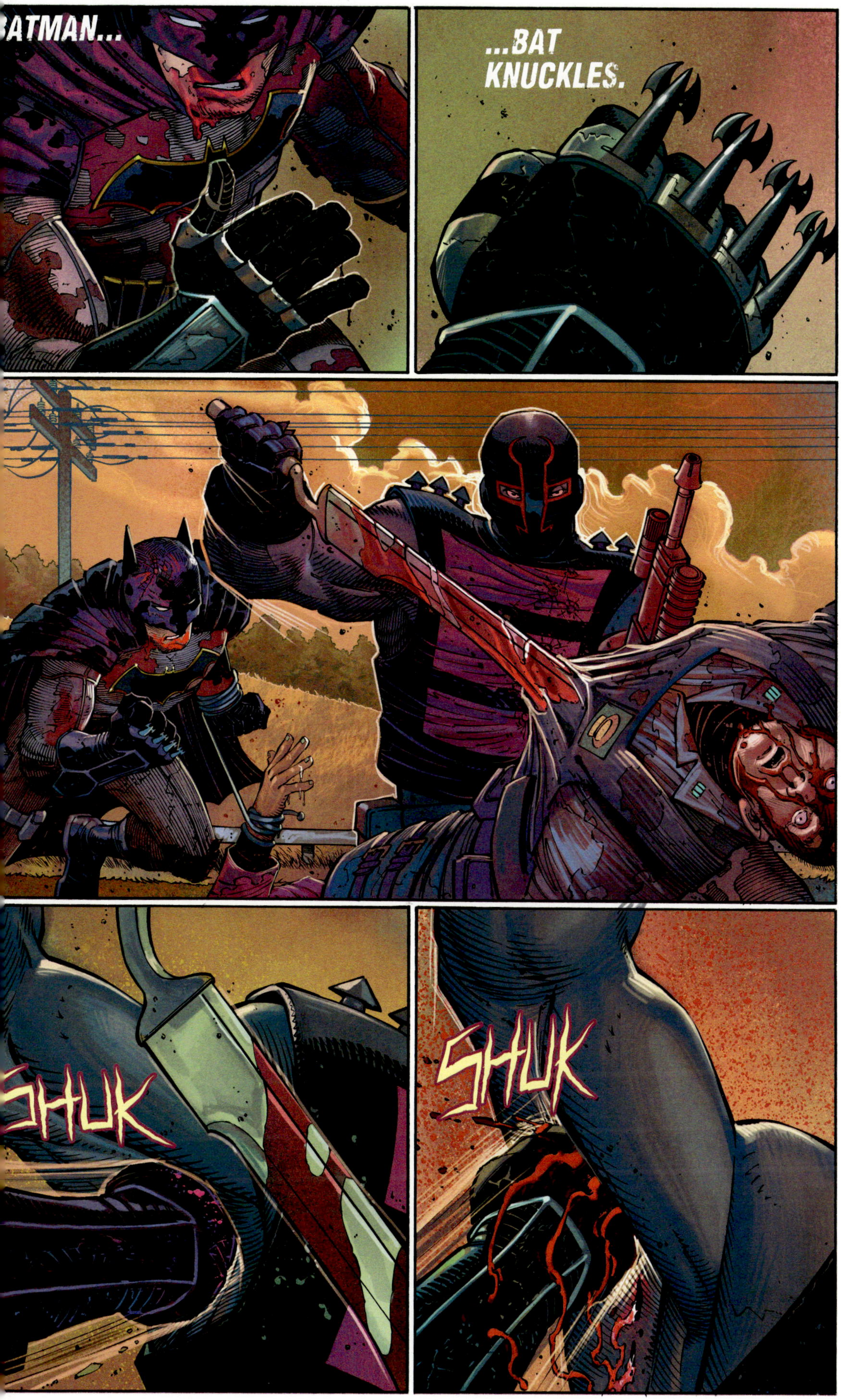

COME ON!
SHUK

CLANG

COUGH COUGH

Unh! NO.

PING
PING

HEY, COMMIE.

THE BAT AND I HAVE A BET GOING, AND YOU--

GAK!

HARVEY!

BATMAN.
MR. DENT.
AS I WAS SAYING, I'D LIKE TO TALK TO YOU ABOUT SOMETHING.
IT'S CALLED *SEA-STEADING.* THE CREATION OF PRIVATE ISLANDS WHERE ONE CAN DO ANYTHING ONE WANTS...
...WITHOUT ANY LAW AT ALL.

KRUNKK

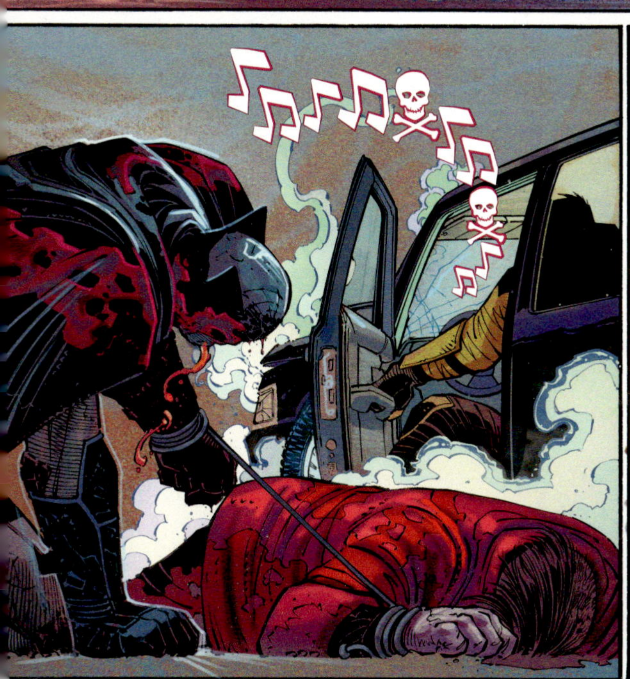

WAIT... ARE THOSE *ACTUAL* CHINESE STARS IN HIS FA--
THEY'RE LODGED IN THREE ARTERIES.
WE NEED TO GET HARVEY TO A SAFE HOUSE O HE'LL DIE. TURN THAT NOISE DOWN!
SORRY. BUT WHAT SAFE HOUSE? WE'RE IN THE MIDDLE OF--
JUST FOLLOW THE ROAD SIGNS.
ROAD SIGNS? WHAT ROAD SIGNS?
RIGHT THERE, DUKE. THAT ONE.
...YOU HAVE TO BE KIDDING ME.

YOU THERE.

WHICH WAY DID THEY GO?

THE ROYAL FLUSH GANG:
A.K.A. MESS.

KUMGGO
K&G
THERE'S MORE, EVIDENTLY.
DBL 00

WE'RE IN OVER OUR HEADS, OSWALD.
SIONIS IS RIGHT. IT'S NOT THE DAMN BLOOD MESS.

IT'S WHAT HE'LL DO TO US WHEN HE REALIZES *WE CAN'T PAY WHAT YOU PROMISED HIM. WHAT THEN?*
LET ME WORRY ABOUT THAT, WARREN. I HAVE A--
HEY, BIRD-MAN.

IF YOU NEED A NEW JOB, YOU CAN BE A *DECOY* FOR US ANYTIME.

YOU LIKE DUCK, DON'T YOU? HAHA!

Heh. SURE, I LIKE DUCK. THING ABOUT DUCK, YOU HAVE TO KNOW HOW TO ***ROAST*** IT.

AND LET
T COOK A
OOD LONG
WHILE.

WE'RE
GETTING
CLOSE!
NOT THE
CAVE ITSELF,
TURN OFF AT THAT
DIRT ROAD UP
AHEAD.
FAMOUS
BAT-CAVE.
LIVE BATS!
1 MILE

HERE,
HERE!
A
WALNUT
FARM,
BUT--
JUST DO IT!
WE NEED TO GET
THESE THINGS
OUT OF HIS FACE
BEFORE HE--
ALL NUT
FARMS

0 MINUTES LATER.
CLINK

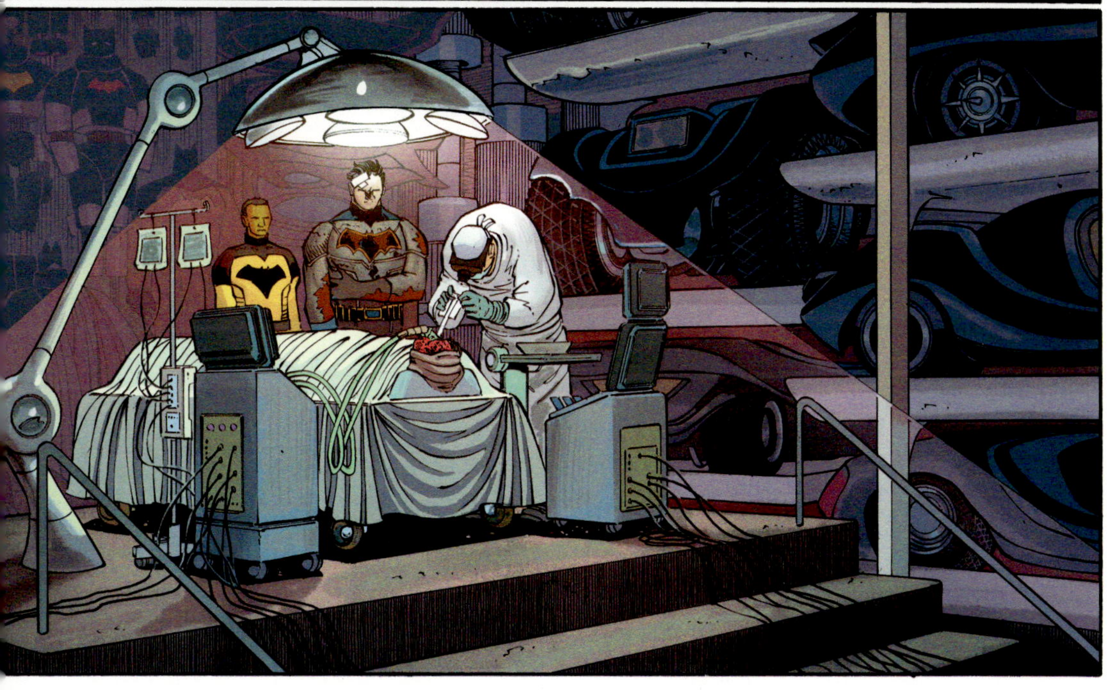

WELL?
HARD TO SAY.

THE NEXT COUPLE HOURS WILL TELL. BUT THE EYE MIGHT NEED TO COME OUT.
THAT MIGHT NOT BE A BAD THING.

HAROLD ALLNUT:
GENIUS INVENTOR.
MUTE. FAMILY.

THANK YOU, OLD FRIEND. IT'S GOOD TO SEE YOU.
THE OLD AQUEDUCT PIPELINE ALLOWS HIM TO SHIP MATERIAL DOWNRIVER.

IT'S GOOD TO MEET YOU, DUKE. WELCOME TO THE RABBLE.

I...IT ISN'T GOOD. WE NEED TRANSPORT UP THE PIPELINE.

OF COURSE. AND I'M SORRY TO HEAR IT'S UGLY. I WAS HOPING...WELL, IT'S EASY TO HOPE FROM DOWN HERE. I'LL SEE WHAT I HAVE.

BRUCE, NEED TO TALK TO YOU.
COMMISSIONER GORDON...HE CALLED THE HOUSE.
THERE'S SOME *FILE* AT THE DEPARTMENT THAT'S GOING TO SELF-DECRYPT IF YOU KEEP UP WITH THIS. SOMETHING THAT CLAIMS TO LINK *BRUCE WAYNE* TO--
WE KEEP GOING.

...
ALL RIGHT. BUT THERE'S SOMETHING ELSE, TOO. I LOOKED AT THE LAST VERSION OF THIS "CURE" HARVEY WAS WORKING ON.
THE MAIN INGREDIENT, *VASOPRINE*--THEY BUILT CURES OUT OF IT FOR PEOPLE INFECTED DURING THE LAST JOKER ATTACK, LIKE MY PARENTS.
IT CURED THEM OF HYPER-MALICE FOR A LITTLE WHILE, BUT ULTIMATELY EVERYONE REVERTED. NONE OF IT HELD.

KNOW ABOUT THE STS. BUT THE *CURE* BE THERE, AT THE HOUSE. I HAVE TO ELIEVE THAT. LIKE I SAID, WE KEEP GOING.
FINE. TELL ME WHY.
I HAVE.
NO, NOT BECAUSE YOU'RE BATMAN AND THAT'S WHAT YOU DO. WHAT IS IT WITH THIS ONE? REALLY. WHAT IS THIS PLACE, THE HOUSE?
...

FINE. I'LL HEAD BACK.
WAIT.
DUKE, LISTEN...

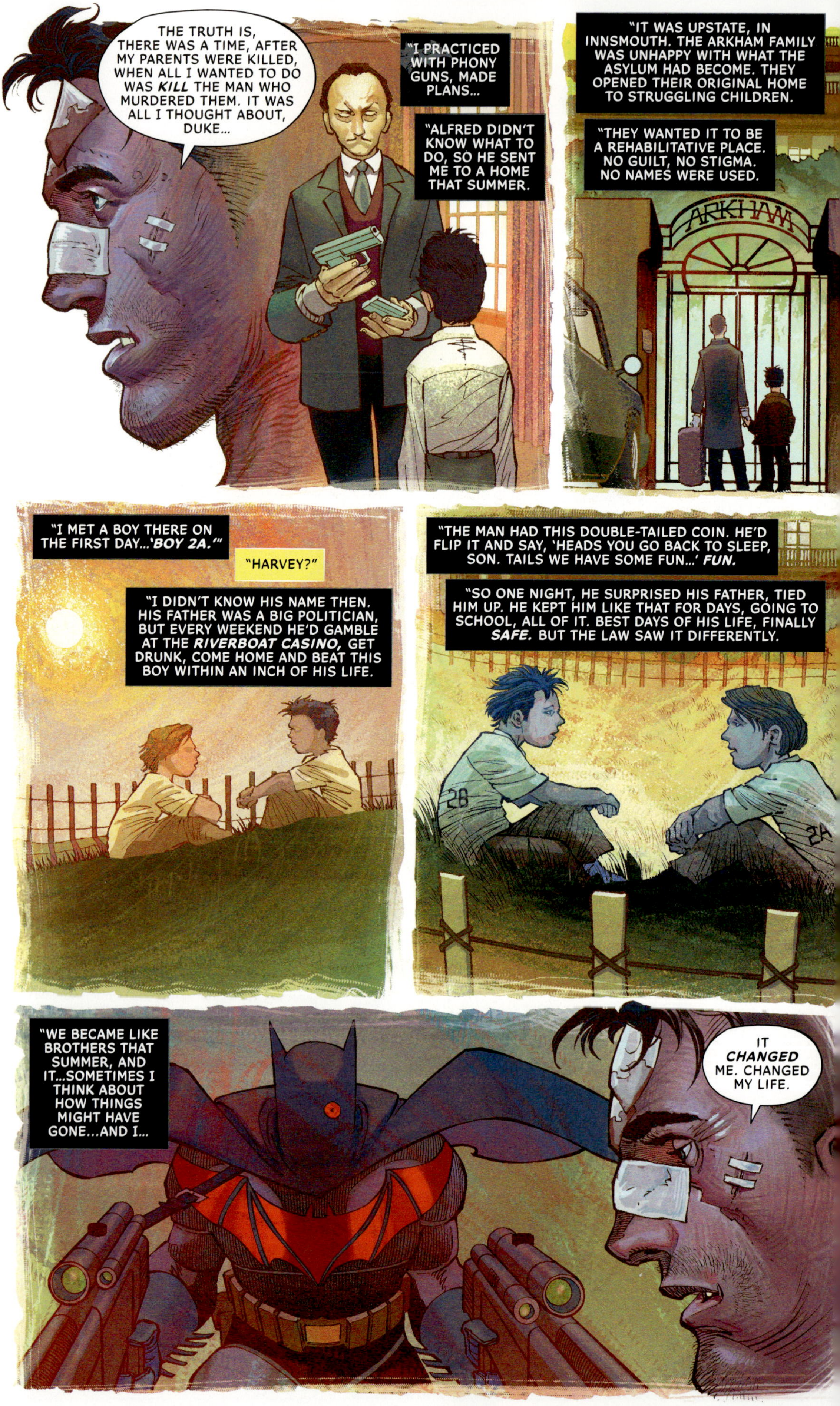

THE TRUTH IS, THERE WAS A TIME, AFTER MY PARENTS WERE KILLED, WHEN ALL I WANTED TO DO WAS ***KILL*** THE MAN WHO MURDERED THEM. IT WAS ALL I THOUGHT ABOUT, DUKE...

"I PRACTICED WITH PHONY GUNS, MADE PLANS...

"ALFRED DIDN'T KNOW WHAT TO DO, SO HE SENT ME TO A HOME THAT SUMMER.

"IT WAS UPSTATE, IN INNSMOUTH. THE ARKHAM FAMILY WAS UNHAPPY WITH WHAT THE ASYLUM HAD BECOME. THEY OPENED THEIR ORIGINAL HOME TO STRUGGLING CHILDREN.

"THEY WANTED IT TO BE A REHABILITATIVE PLACE. NO GUILT, NO STIGMA. NO NAMES WERE USED.

ARKHAM

WHEN WE MET YEARS LATER, WE DIDN'T REALIZE WHO EACH OTHER WAS AT FIRST.
THE HOUSE HAD CLOSED AFTER THAT SUMMER. BUT WE DECIDED WE'D ***REOPEN*** IT. IT WAS GOING TO BE A ***NEW*** ARKHAM. A GOOD PLACE.
BUT THEN, HARVEY...HE BECAME WHAT HE IS AND IT ALL FELL APART.
LOOK, I KNOW THE ODDS HERE, DUKE. I DO. AND I UNDERSTAND IF YOU WANT TO TURN BACK.
I'M ALL ABOUT LONG ODDS, UCE. MY FAVORITE METAL BAND? EY'RE A BUNCH OF EX-ARKHAM INMATES WHO TURNED THEMSELVES AROUND.
O, NO, I'M OT GOING CK. I JUST... EEDED TO HEAR IT.
...
THANK YOU. YOU'RE A GOOD ALLY.
I'M TRYING. I PROMISE.
WAS YOUR BAND THAT NOISE YOU WERE PLAYING IN THE CAR?
THE VERY SAME. CHECK OUT THEIR NAME. HERE.
"BATMAN'S @^$&@"? THAT'S NOT FUNNY.
AW, IT'S PRETTY FUNNY. WAIT, YOU'RE NOT GOING TO SUE THEM OR ANYTHING, RIGHT?
HRM.
"HRM"? WHAT'S "HRM"? BRUCE? BRUCE?

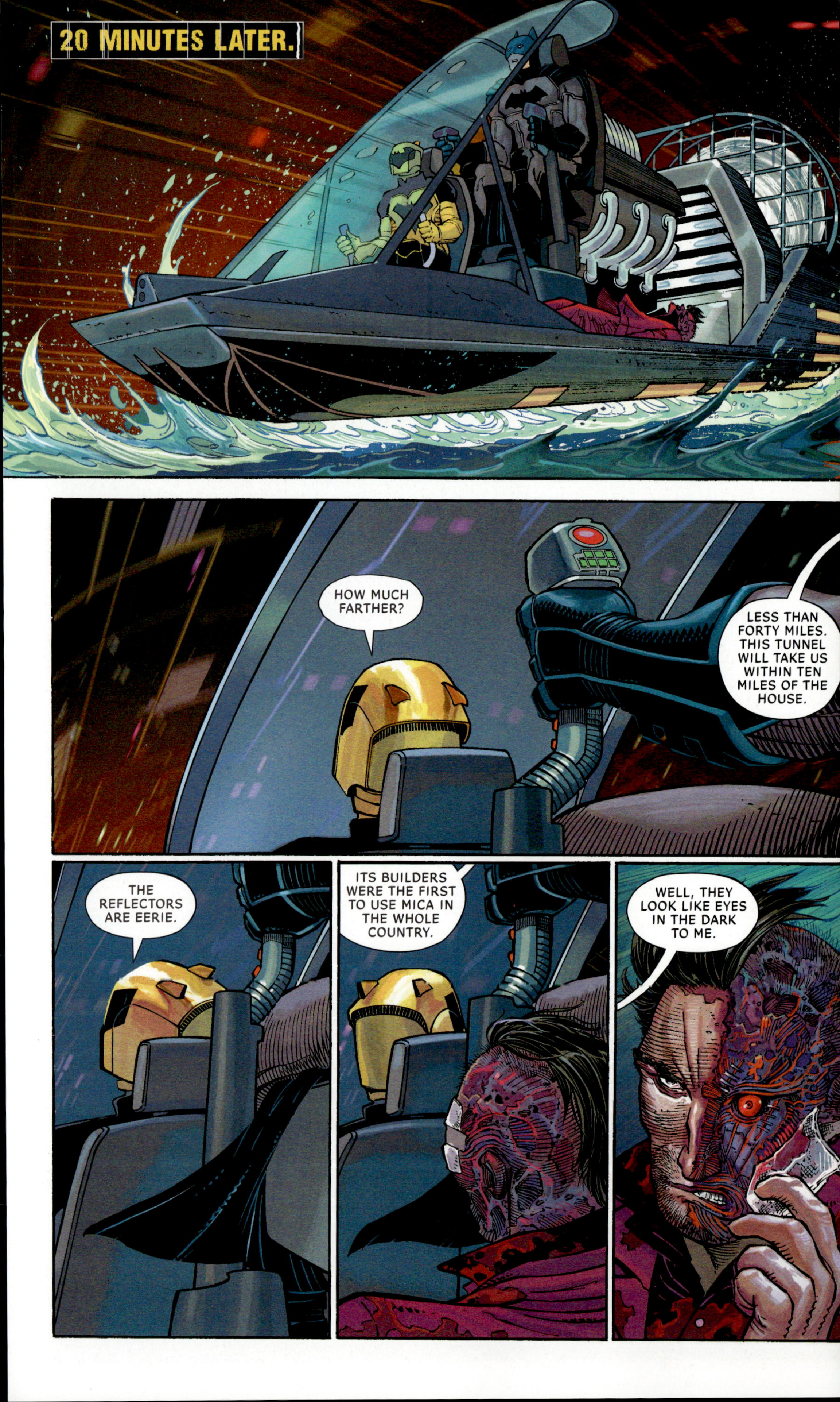

20 MINUTES LATER.

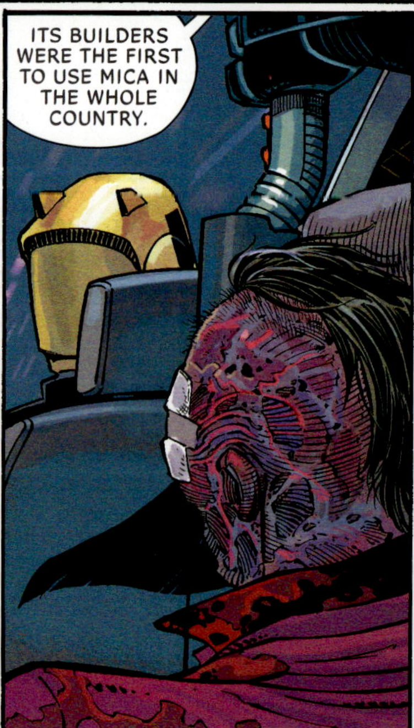

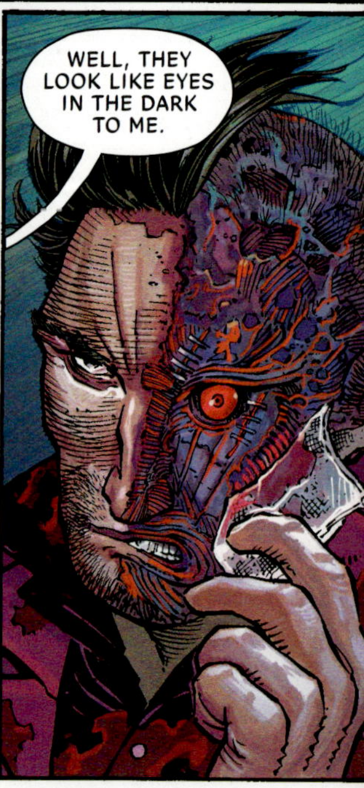

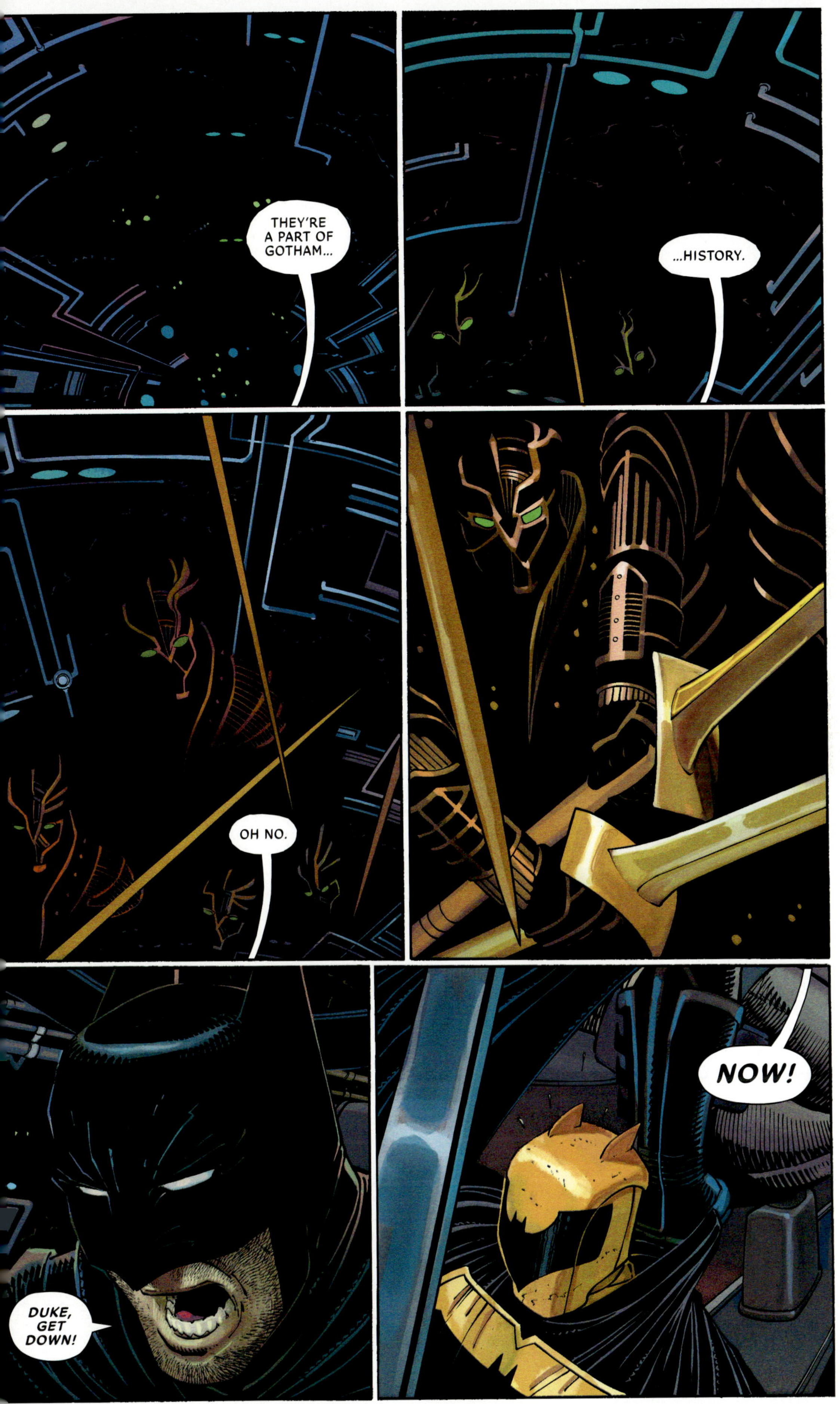
THEY'RE A PART OF GOTHAM...
...HISTORY.
OH NO.
DUKE, GET DOWN!
NOW!

FUNNY THING ABOUT *HISTORY.*
HOW IT ALWAYS ***COMES BACK*** TO HAUNT.

SEE, I HEARD YOUR LITTLE STORY BACK THERE...
TING

AND YOU DIDN'T TELL THE KID THE **WHOLE TRUTH,** DID YOU? YOU SUGARCOATED IT. BECAUSE THAT'S WHAT YOU DO.

BUT I TOLD YOU, BATS, EVERY BIT FARTHER YOU MAKE IT DOWN THE ROAD, EVERY TIME YOU RAISE, I RAISE, TOO.

HARVEY'S IN ME, BUT I'M IN HIM, TOO. DID IT EVER OCCUR TO YOU THAT MAYBE IT WAS **ME** YOU WERE TALKING TO BACK THEN? OR THAT THIS **CURE** YOU'RE AFTER...

...IT'S NOT ABOUT MAKING ME INTO HIM, BUT ABOUT MAKING **HIM** INTO **ME?**
NOT *UNH* POSSIBLE...

I DON'T KNOW...MAYBE THE KID'S RIGHT.
AND MAYBE **YOU** SHOULD STICK A--
AGH!
SHKT

MILES TRAVELED: 222 MILES TO GO: 276

OIN FLIP
SLOT
80
$1
20
15
3
$3
PLAY
OIN FLIP
ACKPOT
JR 16
White

COIN FLIP
SLOT
80
$1
20
15
3
$3
PLAY
COIN FLIP
JACKPOT

MY OWN WORST
ENEMY PART 4

RIGHT NOW.
COTT SNYDER SCRIPT JOHN ROMITA JR. PENCILS
ANNY MIKI INKS DEAN WHITE COLORS STEVE WANDS LETTERS
OMITA, MIKI, WHITE COVER

AVE WIELGOSZ ASSISTANT EDITOR REBECCA TAYLOR ASSOCIATE EDITOR MARK DOYLE EDITOR

HELLO?
IS SOMEONE THERE?
HELP! LET ME OUT! PLEASE! I BEEN DOWN HERE SO LONG. PLEEEEASE! MY NAILS HAVE GROWN THROUGH MY SKIN! I'LL BE GOOD!

"I'LL BE GOOD LIKE EVERYONE ELSE! FOR GOD'S SAKE JUST LET ME OUT!"
ALSO NOW.
YOU WANT OUT, AM I RIGHT, BATMAN?
I KNOW THAT FEELING.
NOOO!
SEE, I REMEMBER THE SENSATION, AS THE ACID HIT, IN THE MILLISECONDS BEFORE THE PAIN STARTED... THE THING ABOUT THE ACID...
IT'S THE VAPORS. RUIN YOUR EYES, BURN THE BLOOD VESSELS IN THEM...

THEN...THEN YOU BREATHE IT IN, KNOWING SOON IT'LL BE BURNING YOUR FLESH, AND THE STING HITS YER LUNGS...
...AND THE FIRE AKES YOUR CHEST JUST WANT TO...
...EXPLODE.
AM I RIGH--
AGH!

STATUS?
COUGH I'M ALL RIGHT. YOU...?
I'M...
I... CAN'T...
HEH. LIKE I SAID, THE VAPORS, BOSS...YOU'RE BLIND, AREN'T YOU?
SLICE HIM TO PIECES, FELLAS.

NICE OF THE COURT OF OWLS TO GIVE ME MY OWN BATTALION, EH, BATS? SEEMS THEY LIKE THEIR *SECRETS* SAME AS ME.
LIKE TO KEEP THEIR ENEMIES FIGHTING BLIND. *HELPLESS.*
PECTORAL SPEAKERS. *GO.*
ECHOLOCATION. *ON.*
SAY "HELPLESS" AGAIN FOR ME, HARVEY. PLEASE?

MAN, WHAT PART OF YOU IS NOT BOOBYTRAPPED?
DON'T ANSWER THAT.
CUTE, BATS. BUT YOU'RE RUNNING OUT OF GADGETS...
...AND OUT OF ROAD.
AND I'M RUNNING OUT OF *PATIENCE.*

THE GREAT THING ABOUT THESE FELLAS? THEY DON'T NEED TO *BREATHE.*

THEY HAVE THIS ONE MANEUVER I JUST LOVE.

I'VE USED IT A *LOT,* ADMITTEDLY, BUT IT NEVER REALLY GETS OLD.

HERE, I'LL SHOW IT TO YOU.

I CALL IT: "CEMENT SHOES."

THE WATER IS COLD, TOO, MAKES THEM FREEZE UP. HEAVIER, TOUGHER. STATUES HOLDING YOU DOWN.

I'D STAY AND WATCH, BUT HEY, I HAVE A BET TO COLLECT ON.

MY VISOR... BATMAN...IT'S CRACKED AND... ACK!
MINE IS, TOO! LISTEN TO ME! TALONS ARE NECROTIC. THEY'RE STRONG, BUT THEIR VASCULAR SYSTEM IS WEAK. WHICH MAKES THEIR EARDRUMS VULNERABLE! UNDERWATER, SOUND HITS HARDER. I'M LINKING US! LOAD YOUR MUSIC AND I CAN USE THE SPEAKERS TO--
CAN'T BREA--COUGH COUGH
LOAD "BATMAN'S #$%" NOW!
LOADING! MAX VOLUME!

COME ON YOU PIECE OF--
--THERRRRE WE GO. ONE BAR...TWO BARS...
THREE BARS.
KLUNK

THIS WAY. WATCH YOUR STEP.
WHERE ARE WE?
TRUTH? NOWHERE. HOW BAD IS YOUR SIGHT?
NOT GOOD. AND THE ECHOLOCATION SYSTEM IS SHORTED. WHAT DO YOU SEE?
A TINY AIRPORT, CROP DUSTERS AND BIPLANES--
BIPLANES? PERFECT. LET'S GO.
WAITWAITWAIT. YOU WANT TO *FLY* A BIPLANE?! BUT YOUR EYES...
THEY SHOULD BE FINE BY THE TIME I NEED THEM TO LAND.
YOU CAN PLAY YOUR MUSIC THE WHOLE WAY.
BRUCE.
THAT SONG ABOUT JUSTICE BEING TEETH ON THE PAVEMENT. I ALMOST LIKED THAT ONE.
BRUCE.
ROCK AND ROLL WILL NEVER DIE. WHEELS UP IN FIVE. COME ON...

ARKHAM
...WE'RE IN THE HOME-STRETCH.
TWO-B... TWO-B!
HEY, YOU UP?
WHAT, TWO-A? WHAT IS IT? WHAT'S WRONG?
IT CAME BACK TO ME. BUT NOT LIKE I THOUGHT...
LOOK INSIDE. LOOK.
BRUCE? DO YOU SEE?

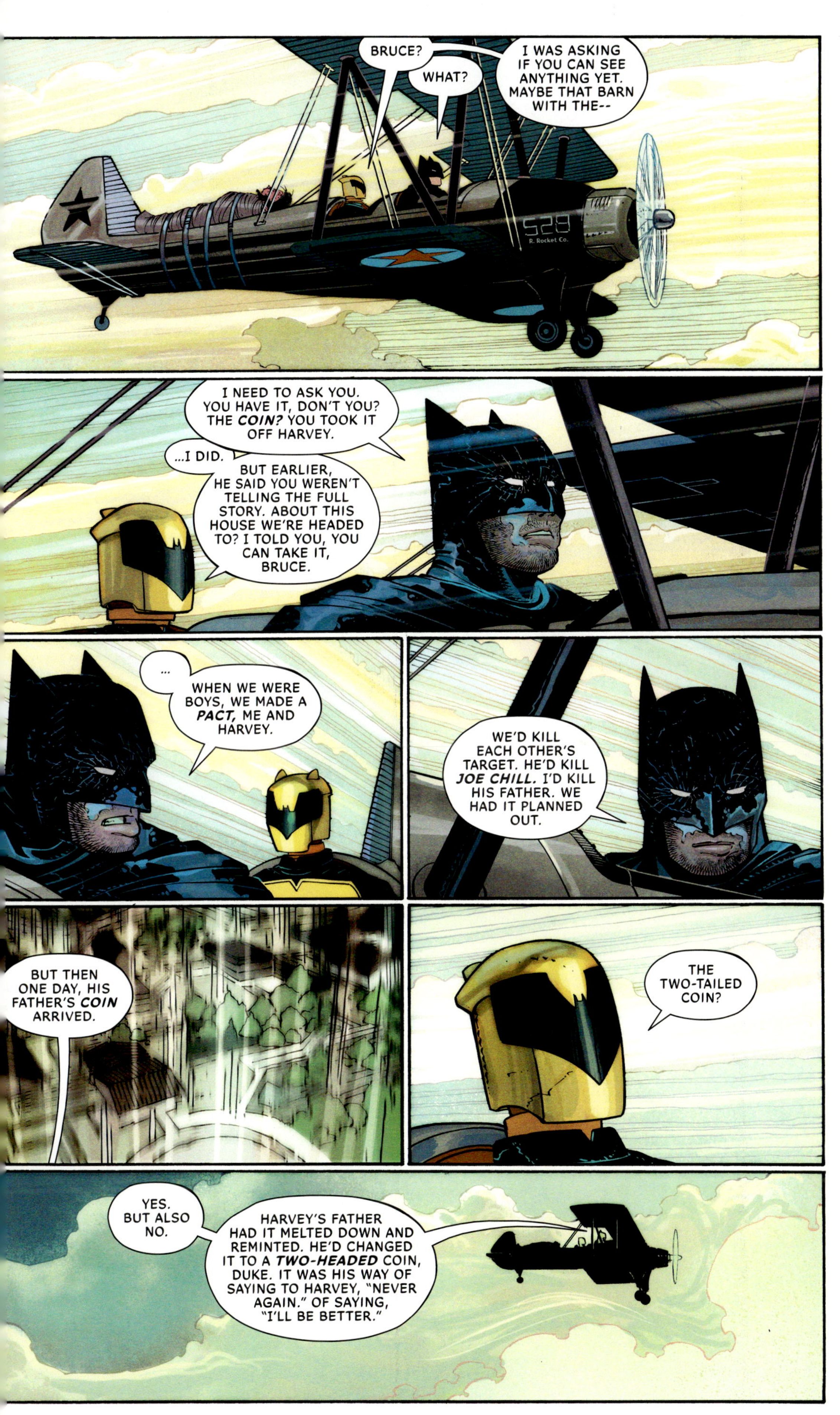
BRUCE?
WHAT?
I WAS ASKING IF YOU CAN SEE ANYTHING YET. MAYBE THAT BARN WITH THE--
528
R. Rocket Co.
I NEED TO ASK YOU. YOU HAVE IT, DON'T YOU? THE *COIN?* YOU TOOK IT OFF HARVEY.
...I DID.
BUT EARLIER, HE SAID YOU WEREN'T TELLING THE FULL STORY. ABOUT THIS HOUSE WE'RE HEADED TO? I TOLD YOU, YOU CAN TAKE IT, BRUCE.
...
WHEN WE WERE BOYS, WE MADE A *PACT,* ME AND HARVEY.
WE'D KILL EACH OTHER'S TARGET. HE'D KILL *JOE CHILL.* I'D KILL HIS FATHER. WE HAD IT PLANNED OUT.
BUT THEN ONE DAY, HIS FATHER'S *COIN* ARRIVED.
THE TWO-TAILED COIN?
YES. BUT ALSO NO.
HARVEY'S FATHER HAD IT MELTED DOWN AND REMINTED. HE'D CHANGED IT TO A *TWO-HEADED* COIN, DUKE. IT WAS HIS WAY OF SAYING TO HARVEY, "NEVER AGAIN." OF SAYING, "I'LL BE BETTER."

SEEING IT...HARVEY... HE CHANGED HIS MIND ABOUT OUR PLAN.
ME? I WAS ANGRIER THAN EVER. THREW THIS NEW TWO-HEADED COIN INTO THE OCEAN, ONCE AND FOR ALL.
"BUT IT WAS TOO LATE. HE'D ALREADY DECIDED TO BELIEVE IN HIS FATHER.
"I REMEMBER SCREAMING AT HARVEY. 'YOU KNOW HE'LL JUST BEAT YOU AGAIN! YOU KNOW IT!
"THE THING IS, HARVEY KNEW I WAS RIGHT. KNEW HIS FATHER WOULD BEAT HIM AGAIN, TORTURE HIM. BUT HE'D CHOSEN TO BELIEVE IN HIM. HE WASN'T SEEING THE WORLD *AS IT WAS,* BUT HOW HE *WOULD MAKE IT.*
"IT'S NOT ANALYSIS. IT'S NOT ACCEPTANCE. IT'S *FORCE OF WILL.*
"WE HAVE TO SEE PEOPLE AS WE KNOW THEY *CAN* BE, DUKE. IT'S TERRIFYING OUT THERE RIGHT NOW. BUT WHEN THEY SHOW UP AT THE END OF THIS TRIP, THEY *WILL* BE HEROES. THEY WILL BE GOOD AND BRAVE AND STRONG OF HEART. THE COIN AS IT IS NOW, SCARRED, IT'S *NOT* HOW I SEE THINGS."
...I GET IT.
MY PARENTS. THEY MOVE AROUND IN THE DARK, SAYING THINGS THAT KILL ME, YOU KNOW?
BUT THE UGLINESS, IT'S THERE, TOO. MAYBE IT'S PART OF WHAT MAKES THEM HEROIC, PUSHING THROUGH. WHEN THEY DO, I MEAN.
I DON'T KNOW.
DUKE.
SORRY. HERE.

MILES TRAVELED: 407 MILES TO GO: 91

THEY SAY NO MAN IS AN ISLAND, BUT I BELIEVE THE OPPOSITE.
WE ARE *ALL* ISLANDS.
AND THAT IS A GOOD THING.
666
ME, I USED TO TELL MYSELF I KILLED BECAUSE I *HAD* TO.
FOR COUNTRY. THEN. FOR SURVIVAL.
BUT I WAS *LYING* TO MYSELF.
THE TRUTH IS, I KILL BECAUSE I *LOVE* TO KILL.
I ASKED YOU EARLIER IF YOU'D HEARD OF ***SEA-STEADING.*** I HAVE BUILT THIS ISLAND MYSELF.
IT EXISTS AT THE SIXTH PARALLEL SOUTH AND 66TH MERIDIAN EAST, JUST OFF THE COAST OF SOUTH AMERICA. ***666.*** THE LOCATION OF THE ***BEAST.*** NO LAW.
I EVE HAVE LOGO. I ON THA KNIFE YOUR RETINA CULUM
I WILL TAKE YOU THERE. FAR FROM THIS PLACE.
SILVER D LLAR
CASINO
I WILL **HUNT** YOU FOR A YEAR.
MAYBE TWO. WE WILL CIRCLE EACH OTHER...
IT WILL BE...A DELIGHT.
BEAST.
ENOUGH ABOUT YOUR PLANS. LET'S TALK ABOUT ***OURS.***

BUT FIRST, A THANK YOU TO BATMAN, FOR BRINGING HARVEY TO US.

HAVE TO SAY, YOU TWO KE DARLING TRAVELING PARTNERS.
HEH. IT'S LIKE THE TWO BROADS WHO GO OFF THE #$%^ CLIFF ALL OVER AGAIN.

JUST MAKING A QUICK PIT STOP. I FIGURE ANYWHERE YOU THREE ARE IS A GOOD PLACE TO TAKE A--

LANGUAGE, MY FRIEND. SO SALTY.
I SUPPOSE OLD HARVEY HAS BEEN RUBBING OFF ON YOU.

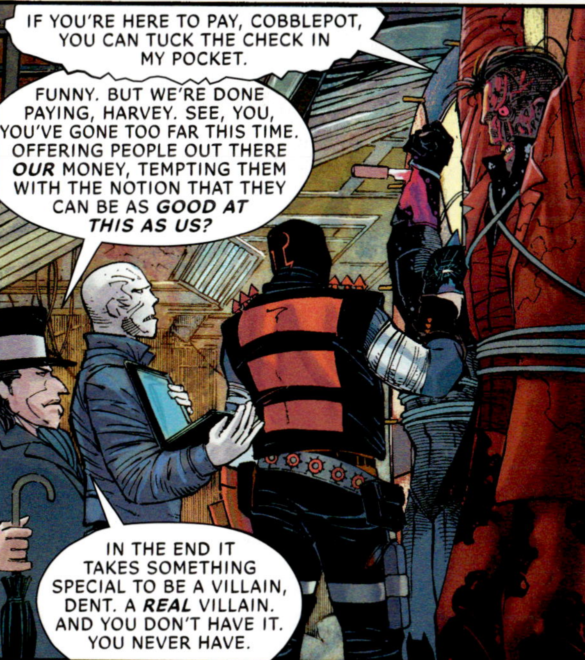
IF YOU'RE HERE TO PAY, COBBLEPOT, YOU CAN TUCK THE CHECK IN MY POCKET.
FUNNY. BUT WE'RE DONE PAYING, HARVEY. SEE, YOU, YOU'VE GONE TOO FAR THIS TIME. OFFERING PEOPLE OUT THERE ***OUR*** MONEY, TEMPTING THEM WITH THE NOTION THAT THEY CAN BE AS ***GOOD AT THIS AS US?***
IN THE END IT TAKES SOMETHING SPECIAL TO BE A VILLAIN, DENT. A ***REAL*** VILLAIN. AND YOU DON'T HAVE IT. YOU NEVER HAVE.

BUT DON'T TAKE MY WORD FOR IT, HARVEY.
TAKE HIS.
HELLO, TWO-FACE.

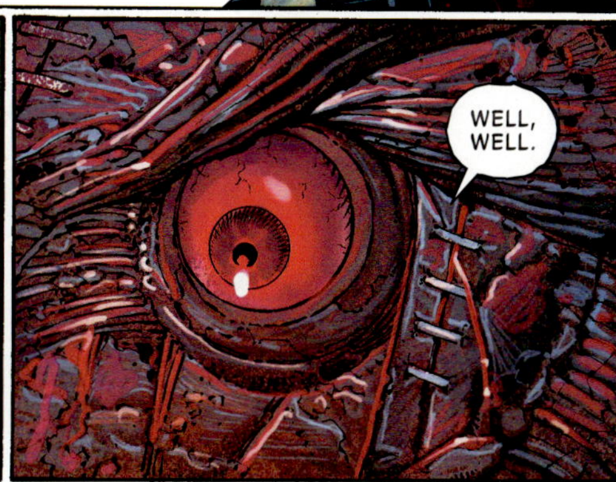
WELL, WELL.

IF YOU'RE SEEING THIS, THAT MEANS BATMAN DIDN'T GET YOU TO WHERE I WAS HOPING HE'D GET YOU.

HARVEY... NO.

THAT'S OKAY, THOUGH. BECAUSE I SET UP A CONTINGENCY PLAN. SEE, BEFORE I CHANGED OVER TO...YOU, I PUT A **TRACKER** IN ME. SO JUST IN CASE YOU GOT AWAY FROM BATMAN... THEY COULD FIND YOU.
NOW, YOU'RE GOING TO GIVE THEM THE CODES TO EVERYTHING YOU HAVE ON EVERYONE, OR THEY'RE GOING TO **KILL** YOU. AND I'M OKAY WITH THAT.
BECAUSE I'M THE STRONGER SIDE, TWO-FACE. YOU **KNOW** IT. IT'S WHY YOU NEVER KILLED OUR FATHER. IT'S WHY YOU KEEP THAT COIN. WHY YOU NEVER TRIED TO GET RID OF ME. BECAUSE DEEP DOWN, YOU HOLD ON TO **HOPE,** JUST LIKE THE GOOD PEOPLE OF THIS STATE.
SO TALK, GIVE UP, OR MY FACE WILL BE THE LAST ONE YOU SEE.

SO THERE YOU HAVE IT. YOU **WANT** TO BE LIKE US. BUT YOU'RE NOT. YOU'RE LIKE EVERYONE OUT THERE. SOFT INSIDE.
NOW, YOU'RE GOING TO TELL US THE CODE TO YOUR LITTLE NETWORK, AND MAYBE, JUST MAYBE, WE'LL MAKE THIS REALLY SLOW.

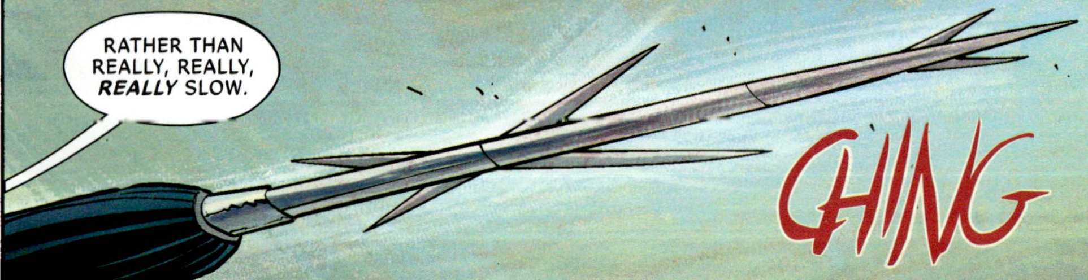
RATHER THAN REALLY, REALLY, **REALLY** SLOW.
CHING

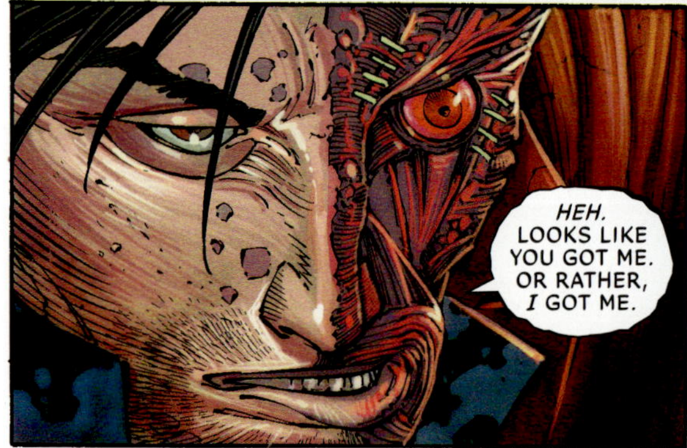
HEH. LOOKS LIKE YOU GOT ME. OR RATHER, *I* GOT ME.

GOOD. SO. PASSWORD.

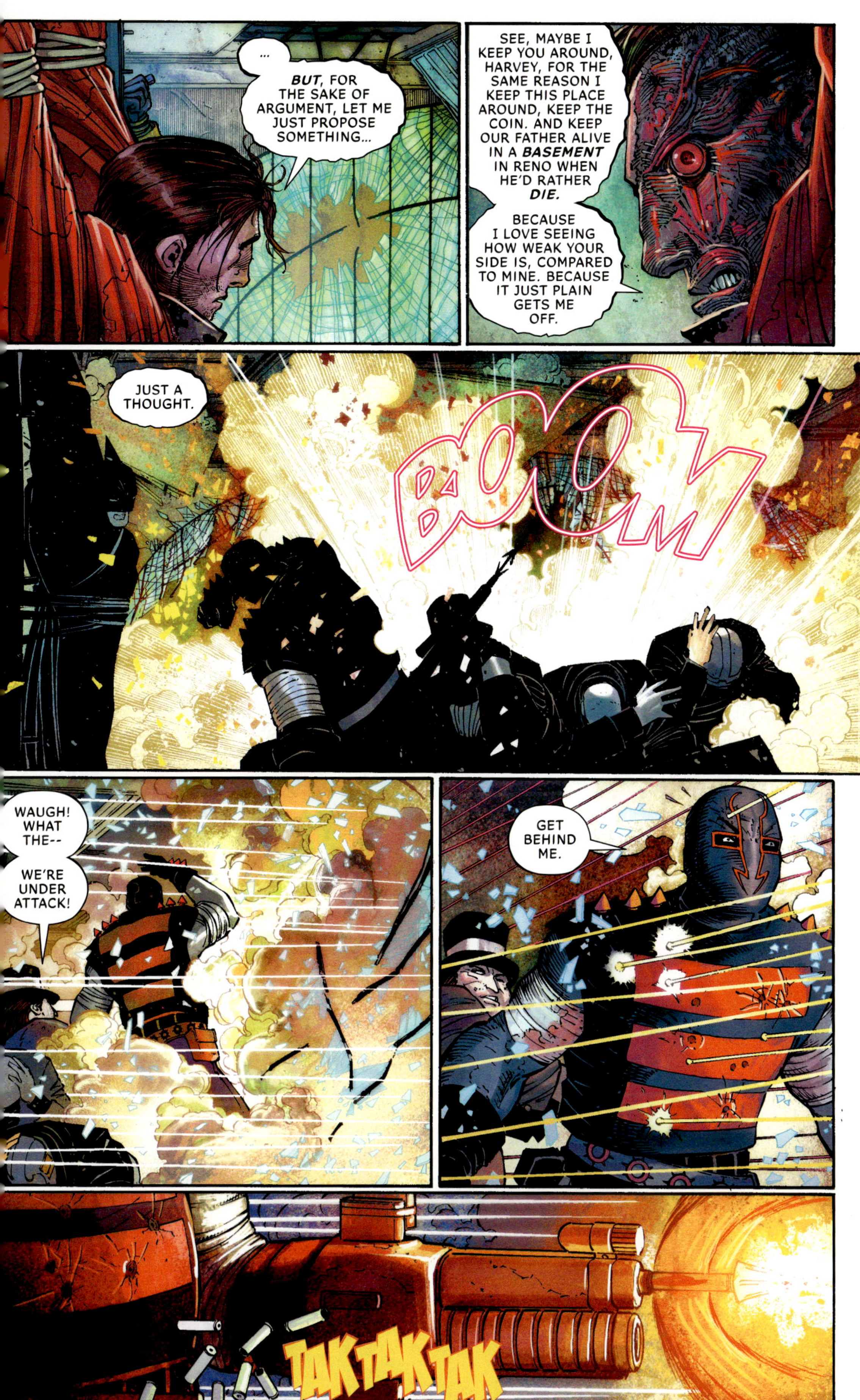
...
BUT, FOR THE SAKE OF ARGUMENT, LET ME JUST PROPOSE SOMETHING...
SEE, MAYBE I KEEP YOU AROUND, HARVEY, FOR THE SAME REASON I KEEP THIS PLACE AROUND, KEEP THE COIN. AND KEEP OUR FATHER ALIVE IN A BASEMENT IN RENO WHEN HE'D RATHER DIE.
BECAUSE I LOVE SEEING HOW WEAK YOUR SIDE IS, COMPARED TO MINE. BECAUSE IT JUST PLAIN GETS ME OFF.
JUST A THOUGHT.
BOOM
WAUGH! WHAT THE--
WE'RE UNDER ATTACK!
GET BEHIND ME.
TAK TAK TAK

RRRR...
RAAAHH!
COME ON!
WHO DID YOU CALL?!
TELL ME!
WHO THE HELL IS OUT THERE? *DEATHSTROKE?* SHIVA? WHO?!
AW, ALL I DID WAS SEND OUT THE *TRACKER CODE* THAT HARVEY SENT TO COBBLEPOT A BIT WIDER. THAT'S WHAT I WAS DOING WHEN YOU CLOCKED ME BY THE AIRPORT.

THEY'RE GETTING AWAY! AFTER THEM!
DUKE, WHO'S OUT THERE? CAN YOU SEE?
DUKE!
IT'S...JUST PEOPLE.
.IKE YOU SAID, BATS: THEY WILL BE HEROES. THEY WILL BE GOOD AND BRAVE AND STRONG OF HEART," RIGHT? WASN'T THAT WHAT YOU SAID?
DUKE, THEY'RE HERE TO HELP, RIGHT?
BRUCE, EVERYONE OUT THERE, THEY'RE...

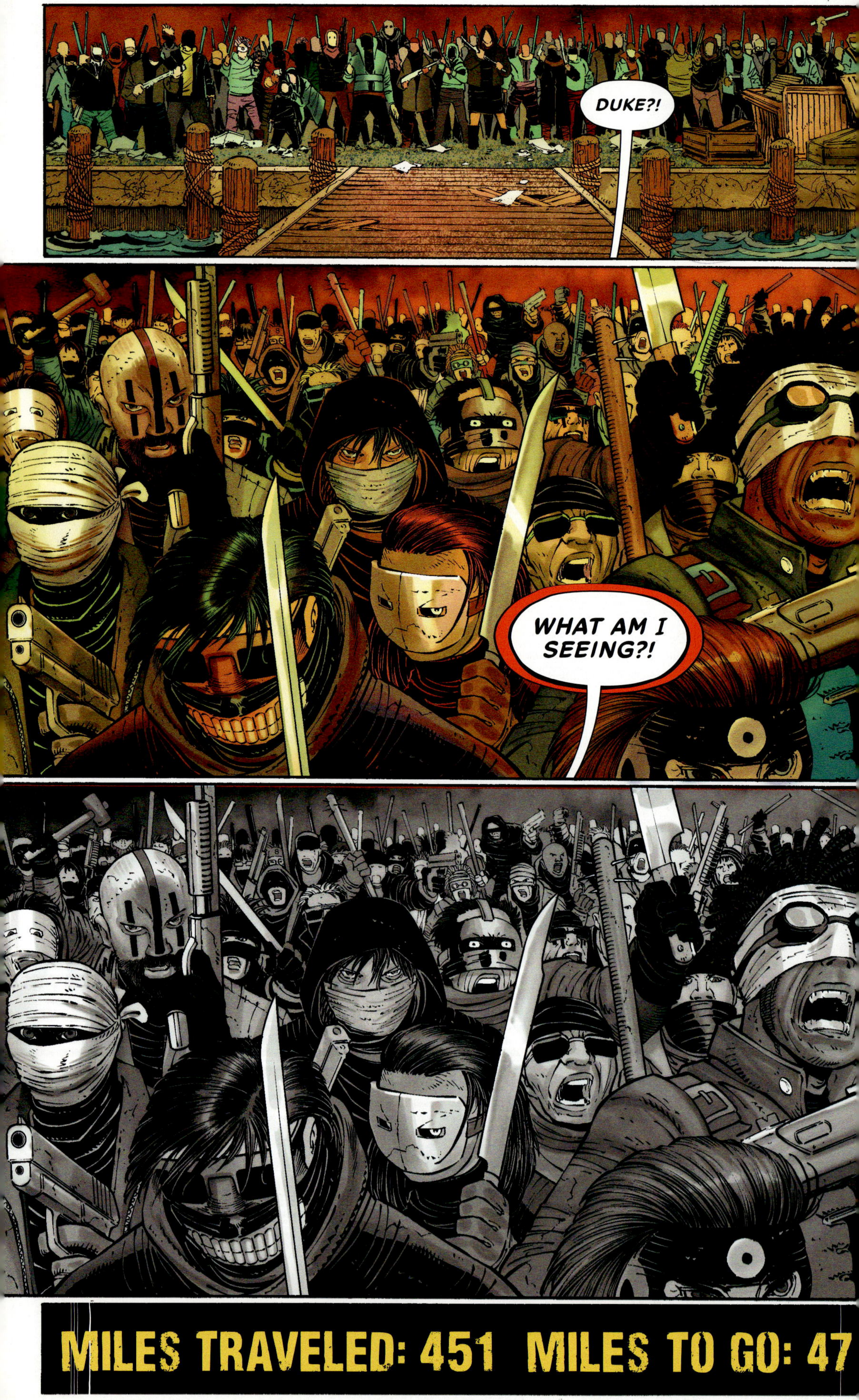

WHAT AM I SEEING?!

MILES TRAVELED: 451 MILES TO GO: 47

JR JR
16
DW

RIGHT NOW.
NOT RIGHT NOW...
DENT AND BATMAN!
THEY'RE INSIDE!
TEAR IT APART! GET THE BAT!
MOVE! I NEED THIS!
THEY'RE ATTACKING *US?!* THEY THINK *THEY* CAN SHOOT IN OUR DIRECTION?! LITTLE, FOUL WEATHER...*KILL THEM, ANATOLI!* KILL THEM ALL!

WITH PLEASURE.
CHICKCHICK
BOOM
WHAT THE... WE'RE MOVING! WHY ARE WE MOVING?!

BATMAN. HE BLEW THE MOORING. WE ARE ADRIFT.
ADRIFT?! WELL, WHERE THE HELL DOES THIS DAMN RIVER GO ANYWAY?
O YOU HEAR RUMBLING?
WE'RE HEADED FOR THE #@+&, =&$, ^%© FALLS.
IMPOSSIBLE! OUT OF MY WAY! ANATOLI! USE YOUR TELESCOPE TO SEE! ANATOLI?!
DUKE, SECOND DECK! GO!
THERE AREN'T ANY LIFEBOATS UP THERE, YOU ORON! THIS BOAT ASN'T SUPPOSED O GO ANYWHERE! BUT YOU HAD TO--
I'M NOT AFTER A LIFEBOAT.
THE GAMBLING CHIP?
IT'S FIBERGLASS. I SAW IT WHEN WE CAME ON.
IT'S THE LIGHTEST, MOST BUOYANT MATERIAL ON THIS THING!
COME ON! WE CAN OUTRUN THEM IF--

BUDDA BUDDA

ANATOLI! FORGET THEM! WE'RE HEADED TOWARD THE FALLS! BEAST! *BEAST!*

LOOK OUT!

THOSE PEOPLE, THEY WERE MINE TO KILL, BATMAN. NOW, MY THOUGHTS ON HUNTING YOU HAVE... EXPANDED.
WHIRRR CLICK

HE'S SWITCHING TO V-FORTIES! MINI-GRENADES. DUKE, HARVEY! ALL WE HAVE, TOGETHER, RIGHT...

...NOW!

UNH!

YOU CAN RUN, BUT I MARKED YOU WITH MY BLADE, BATMAN!
CASINO
SILVER
YOU HEAR ME? I MARKED YOU!
GET DOWN!
THE BOAT WON'T TURN!
DAMMIT, ANATOLI! WE'RE ALL GOING TO DIE! HELP US, YOU ONE-ARMED, VODKA-SOAKED--
LEAN LEFT! NOW! CUT HIS ANGLE!
THIS MARK MEANS THIS WILL NEVER END, BATMAN. COUNTRIES CAN FALL, BUT YOU AND I, WE ARE INSIDE SOMETHING NOW! SOMETHING VERY SPECIAL!
LOOK! WE'RE CHANGING COUR--
NO! WE'RE STILL HEADED RIGHT FOR THE FALLS! WE'RE JUST SPINNING!

OTHER SIDE! LEAN RIGHT!
WHAT THE HELL'S IT MATTER?! WE'RE ALL GOING OVER THE FALLS!
BUDDA BUDDA
NOT ALL OF US.
BOOOM
WHAT WAS THAT?! THE BAT--
WHATEVER IT WAS, WE'RE VEERING! LOOK!
WE'RE HEADED RIGHT FOR--

WAUGH!
CRASH
YOU'RE JUST TRADING UP, YOU KNOW. I'VE SEEN WHAT A BIG DROP INTO WATER DOES TO A PERSON.
ANY OPENING IN YOUR BODY? WATER PUNCHES THROUGH AND RIPS THINGS APART INSIDE. YOUR EYES, MOUTH, EARS AND, YES, EVEN YOUR DAMN--
WE GET IT!

SO. BATMAN...

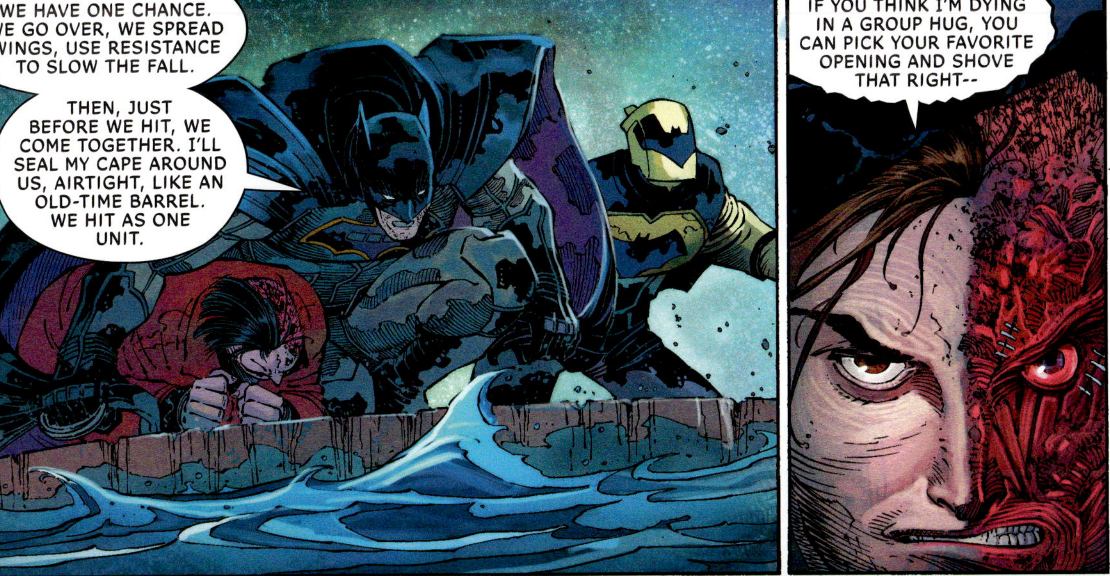
WE HAVE ONE CHANCE. WE GO OVER, WE SPREAD WINGS, USE RESISTANCE TO SLOW THE FALL.
THEN, JUST BEFORE WE HIT, WE COME TOGETHER. I'LL SEAL MY CAPE AROUND US, AIRTIGHT, LIKE AN OLD-TIME BARREL. WE HIT AS ONE UNIT.
IF YOU THINK I'M DYING IN A GROUP HUG, YOU CAN PICK YOUR FAVORITE OPENING AND SHOVE THAT RIGHT--

CRUNCH CRUNCH
CRUNCH
CRUNCH
UMFREE TWEED AND DEEVER TWEED.
.K.A. TWEEDLE DEE AND TWEEDLE DUM.
OOT SOLDIERS FOR THE WONDERLAND GANG.
DUM
DEE
WAIT. ARE WE BEING TOO LOUD?

DEE AND DUM CAME IN A VEHICLE. IT HAS TO BE AROUND HERE...
THERE COULD BE MORE VILLAINS AROUND. OR MORE PEOPLE, IF THEY LOCKED ON TO THE SIGNAL FROM TWO-FACE.
THERE SHOULDN'T BE ANYONE FOLLOWIN US PAST HERE. I TO CARE OF THE TRACKER.
HEH. TRACKER, NO TRACKER. THEY'LL KEEP COMING, PALLLLL...PEOPLE, "VILLAINSSSS"...COUGH
HE DOESN'T LOOK GOOD. WHAT'S WRONG WITH HIM? WAS IT THE FALL?
I DON'T LOOK GOOD? TAKE A LOOK IN THE MIRROR, YOU BAT-MIDGET. YOU PISS-COLORED LITTLE--
ENOUGH.
...
IT'S HARVEY, ISN'T IT?
HE'S COMING BACK. MAYBE IT'S THE INJURIES, MAYBE IT'S THE FACT THAT WE'RE CLOSE TO WHERE WE'RE GOING, BUT HE'S COMING BACK.
HEH! YOU WISHHHH. HARVEY'S NOT COMING BACK... NOT YET. IT'S MY TIME COUGH BESIDES, RIGHT NOW, JIM GORDON IS HEADED TO WAYNE MANOR ON A MISSION. YOU'RE GOING TO LOSE ON ALL FRONTS, BATS... COUGH COUGH...
DUKE, TAKE HIS ARM. I THINK I SEE THE CAR THOSE TWO IDIOTS CAME IN UP AHEAD...
COUGH
GLASS
GLASSWORKS
NICE. VERY INCONSPICUOUS. COULDN'T HAVE BEEN ROXY ROCKET. OR CATMAN. I'LL BET CATMAN HAS A NICE RIDE.
HE DOES NOT. BESIDES, IT DOESN'T MATTER...

..WE'RE ALMOST AT THE END."

EASY THERE.
NO! YOU HAVE NO RIGHT!

THAT'S WHERE YOU'RE WRONG, MR. PENNYWORTH. WE'RE HERE ON ORDERS FROM CITY HALL. AND WE WILL CARRY THOSE ORDERS OUT.
RINGRING

MR. MAYOR? YES. YES, THERE'S A PASSAGE BEHIND THE *CLOCK.* BUT IF ALL THIS IS WHAT IT APPEARS TO BE, I'M CONCERNED ABOUT BOOBY TRAPS. WE'LL NEED THE "BOMB," AND I'LL NEED GEAR.
NO, I WANT TO GO DOWN MYSELF.
ALL RIGHT. SOON AS SUPPLIES ARRIVE.

PLEASE. COMMISSIONER GORDON. JIM... MASTER BRUCE HAS BEEN AN ALLY OF THE POLICE FOR YEARS. HIS DONATIONS, HIS PROGRAMS...
WHATEVER TWO-FACE HAS ON HADY--
ENOUGH!
SCHWARTZ

GET OUT OF HERE, MR. PENNYWORTH. NOW.
HAMAMOTO

PLEASE! PLEASE DON'T DO THIS! IT'LL ONLY--
SHUT UP!

SHUT UP AND LISTEN TO ME. NOW, YOU GO FIND A QUIET SPOT AND *CALL HIM*, FOR GOD'S SAKE. I DON'T KNOW WHAT'S TRUE, YOU HEAR ME? I NEVER HAVE.
BUT EITHER WAY, YOU CALL HIM AND GET HIM TO DO WHATEVER HE HAS TO DO TO TURN THIS BACK. YOU TELL HIM HE HAS ONE CHANCE. CALL HIM!

BUT...MASTER BRUCE IS...OUT OF REACH. I CAN'T...
THEN I'M SORRY. THIS ALL ENDS HERE, TONIGHT.

PENNYWORTH STAYS OUT. LOCK THE DOORS!

THIS IS IT.
MILES TRAVELED: 498 MILES LEFT TO GO:

COME ON. LET'S DO THIS.
HANG ON. I JUST...I JUST WANT TO SAY I WON'T HOLD IT AGAINST YOU IF YOU DON'T GO THROUGH WITH THIS.
WHAT?

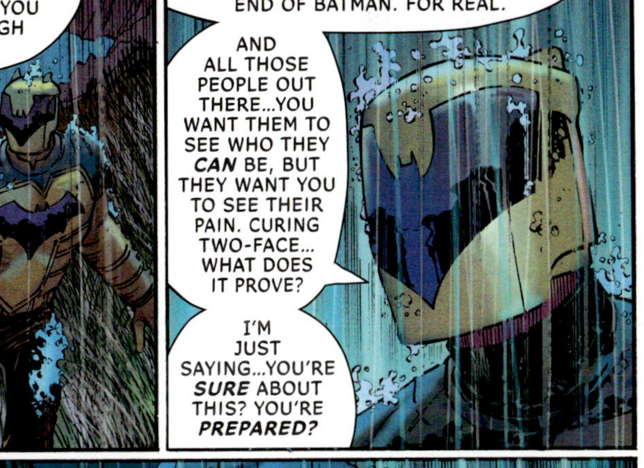
LOOK, I'M *WITH* YOU, BRUCE. BUT THIS...THINK ABOUT IT. IT'LL MEAN THE END OF BATMAN. FOR REAL.
AND ALL THOSE PEOPLE OUT THERE...YOU WANT THEM TO SEE WHO THEY *CAN* BE, BUT THEY WANT YOU TO SEE THEIR PAIN. CURING TWO-FACE... WHAT DOES IT PROVE?
I'M JUST SAYING...YOU'RE *SURE* ABOUT THIS? YOU'RE ***PREPARED?***

"PREPARED?" YES.
"SURE?"
...
LIKE, I SAID, LET'S DO THIS.

HEH. ALL RIGHT THEN. SO YOU CALLLLL?

YES, HARVEY, I DO.
HERE. NOW. I CALL.

SO THIS IS GOOD-BYE.
I GUESS SO.
...
LISTEN, WE PROBABLY WON'T EVER SEE EACH OTHER AGAIN, AND I DON'T EVEN KNOW YOUR NAME, SO...I JUST WANT TO SAY I'M...I'M SORRY I THREW YOUR COIN AWAY. REALLY. WHAT YOU DID FOR ME HERE--
HEY. IT'LL COME BACK SOMEDAY. I BELIEVE IN HIM, YOU KNOW? AND IN ME, AND YOU, TOO, TWO-B. NO MATTER WHAT HAPPENS.
BATMAN?
COMING.

WHERE
IT? THE
CURE.
SO WHERE?
HARVEY HAD TO HIDE IT SO TWO-FACE COULDN'T FIND IT. TWO-FACE MIGHT GUESS THE CURE WAS HERE SOMEWHERE IN THIS HOUSE, BUT FOR ALL HE KNEW, IT WAS HIDDEN OUTSIDE IN THE CLIFFS BY THE BEACH.

TWO UP FROM OUR OLD ROOM, AND TWO OVER. TWO-A PLUS TWO-B. IN HERE.
SIGH
...PLEASE, HARVEY...

...PLEASE...

IT'S HERE.

WE JUST NEED TO TEST IT, MAKE SURE...

...IT WORKS HOW WE...

...WANT...
IT'S GOOD, RIGHT? IT WORKS?
...
HUH... WHERE... WE'RE... HERE?
BRUCE?
HARVEY...
HOW... HOW COULD YOU?
I'M SO SORRY, BRUCE...I KNOW IT'S NOT A CURE, LIKE WE'D HOPED, BUT IT'S A *RESOLUTION* AT LEAST.
IT WORKS ON THE MEOA, ON OXYTOCIN...ON THE *CHEMISTRY* THAT MAKES US COMPASSIONATE OR SELFISH.
IT BURNS AWAY THE WEAKER ELEMENTS WITH NEURO-ACIDS, SO ANYONE WHO TAKES IT, THEY BECOME FULLY ONE OR THE OTHER... AN ALTRUIST OR A SOCIOPATH. ALL BASED ON WHICH SIDE IS STRONGER IN THEM.
HEH. SO WHAT YOU'RE SAYING, HARV, IS THAT IF YOU'RE STRONGER, THEN YOU'LL BE THE *PERMANENT* RESIDENT HERE. IF I AM...WELL, THERE YOU GO.
LOOK AT THIS. SEE, BRUCE? I WARNED YOU. THE FURTHER YOU GO, THE *WORSE* IT'LL GET. AND YOU GET WHERE THIS IS GOING RIGHT, DETECTIVE?
I WASN'T THE ONE WHO DROPPED ACID RAIN ON GOTHAM.
HE WAS.

"THE ACID RAIN, IT WAS A TEST...AND TO MAKE OU THINK *HE* WAS BEHIND IT...IT WAS SUPPOSED TO BE DILUTED, BUT I...HE...I DIDN'T MEAN TO HURT ANYONE, BRUCE. IF I HURT ANYONE..."
"YOU HURT PLENTY."
NO BULL
NO PARKING
"I'M SORRY FOR THAT, BUT YOU NEED TO LISTEN TO ME. I'VE SEEDED THE CLOUDS FOR REAL THIS TIME. THEY'RE LOADED WITH THIS CURE.
"AND IF YOU DON'T GIVE ME MY CURE NOW, IT'LL RAIN DOWN ON ALL OF GOTHAM."
HA. AND WE GET A CITY OF LOVERS OR KILLERS. NOW THAT'S A REAL BET. I'M STARTING TO LIKE YOU, HARV.
I'M...I'M SORRY, BRUCE. TRULY. BUT PLEASE... DO IT. CURE ME. I KNOW I'M WEAKER THAN HIM BUT I... I CAN'T FIGHT ANYMORE.
CURE YOU? THIS ISN'T A CURE. IT'S A *SURRENDER!* AFTER ERYTHING YOU FOUGHT OR...AND THIS IS WHAT OU WANT, TWO-FACE? I THOUGHT YOU LOVED TORMENTING--
I DIDN'T WANT IT THIS WAY, BUT YOU DIDN'T LISTEN TO ME, DID YOU?
AND I NEED GOTHAM MORE THAN I NEED HIM, AND THERE'S NO MORE ROAD HERE. SO DO IT! GET RID OF THIS COWARD INSIDE ME SO WE CAN GET BACK TO NORMAL!
YOU NEED MORE MOTIVATION, PAL? ALL RIGHT. HE MADE HIS PLAN, I MADE MINE.
HERE.
I IMAGINE THIS WAS TO CALL OFF YOUR ATTACK, HARV. BUT LET'S LET BRUCE PHONE HOME FIRST, SHALL WE?
ALFRED?
MASTER BRUCE? THEY'RE HERE! THEY'RE HEADED DOWN TO THE CAVE!
UNKNOWN
AND IT'S... IT'S MY FAULT, SIR. I'M SO SORRY!

YOUR FAULT?

I...I HAD NO CHOICE, SIR. HE TOLD ME THAT IF I DIDN'T BRING THE PLANE DOWN, HE'D ***EXPOSE*** YOU ON THE SPOT.

HE HAS THE PROOF. AND HE SAID THAT IF YOU GOT TO THAT HOUSE...THE ONLY THING WAITING WAS DISAPPOINTMENT AND DEATH...

SO YOU--

HE ***NEVER*** LIES! BUT IF I BROUGHT YOU DOWN SAFELY, AND I EXPLAINED THE SITUATION TO YOU, I THOUGHT...YOU MIGHT TURN BACK.

WHAT DOES HE HAVE ON YOU? TELL ME.

IT WAS WHEN YOU WERE STARTING OUT...I APPROACHED SOMEONE TO...STOP ***HIM***, ONCE AND FOR ALL. JUST HIM...

HIM.

YES, I CAME TO MY SENSES WITHIN HOURS, THOUGH, AND CALLED IT OFF. BUT TWO-FACE, HE WAS ALREADY AWARE...

AND THE WORST PART IS I...I'D...

...USED THE GHOST FUND WE'D ALLOCATED FOR THE ***CAVE***, AND IT ALLOWED TWO-FACE INTO OUR FINANCIAL DATA...

I DIDN'T KNOW, BUT HE LEARNED HOW THE CAVE WAS BEING EXTENDED FROM THE CLOCK. HE GOT THE DESIGNS...

IT'S MY FAULT. ALL BECAUSE I DID THE VERY THING I CHASTISED YOU FOR DOING AS A BOY--PLANNING TO ELIMINATE SOMEONE YOU SAW AS ***EVIL***...I AM A ***HYPOCRITE***. BUT KNOW THAT AT EVERY STAGE, I WAS JUST TRYING TO ***SAVE*** YOU.

SAVE ME? YOU THOUGHT I'D TURN BACK TO PROTECT MYSELF? YOU THOUGHT I'D EVER--

YOU'RE MY SON, FOR GOD'S SAKE! TO IMAGINE YOU SITTING IN JAIL FOR THE REST OF YOUR LIFE? EVERY CRIMINAL YOU HELPED CATCH NOW POSSIBLY SET FREE?

TO SEE YOU TURNED INTO THE CITY'S VILLAIN? NO. BRUCE, THIS TIME, YOU JUST NEED TO GIVE YOURSELF OVER TO...YOU NEED TO DO THIS THING.

PLEASE, BRUCE...OUR FATHER, HE ONCE SAID IN A SPEECH THAT BEING A ***HERO***...IT'S PUTTING WHAT EVERYONE ELSE WANTS BEFORE WHAT ***YOU*** WANT.
...AND BEING A ***VILLAIN*** IS PUTTING WHAT YOU WANT BEFORE ***ALL ELSE.*** I REMEMBER, TOO. BUT IF THAT'S TRUE, BATS, IT SEEMS ***YOU'RE*** ACTUALLY THE REAL BAD GUY OF THIS STORY...AREN'T YOU?

LISTEN TO US, BRUCE. DO THIS. IT'S WHAT EVERYONE WANTS. ME, HIM, EVERYONE OUT THERE...BE THE HERO.

...

WHAT THE HELL ARE YOU--

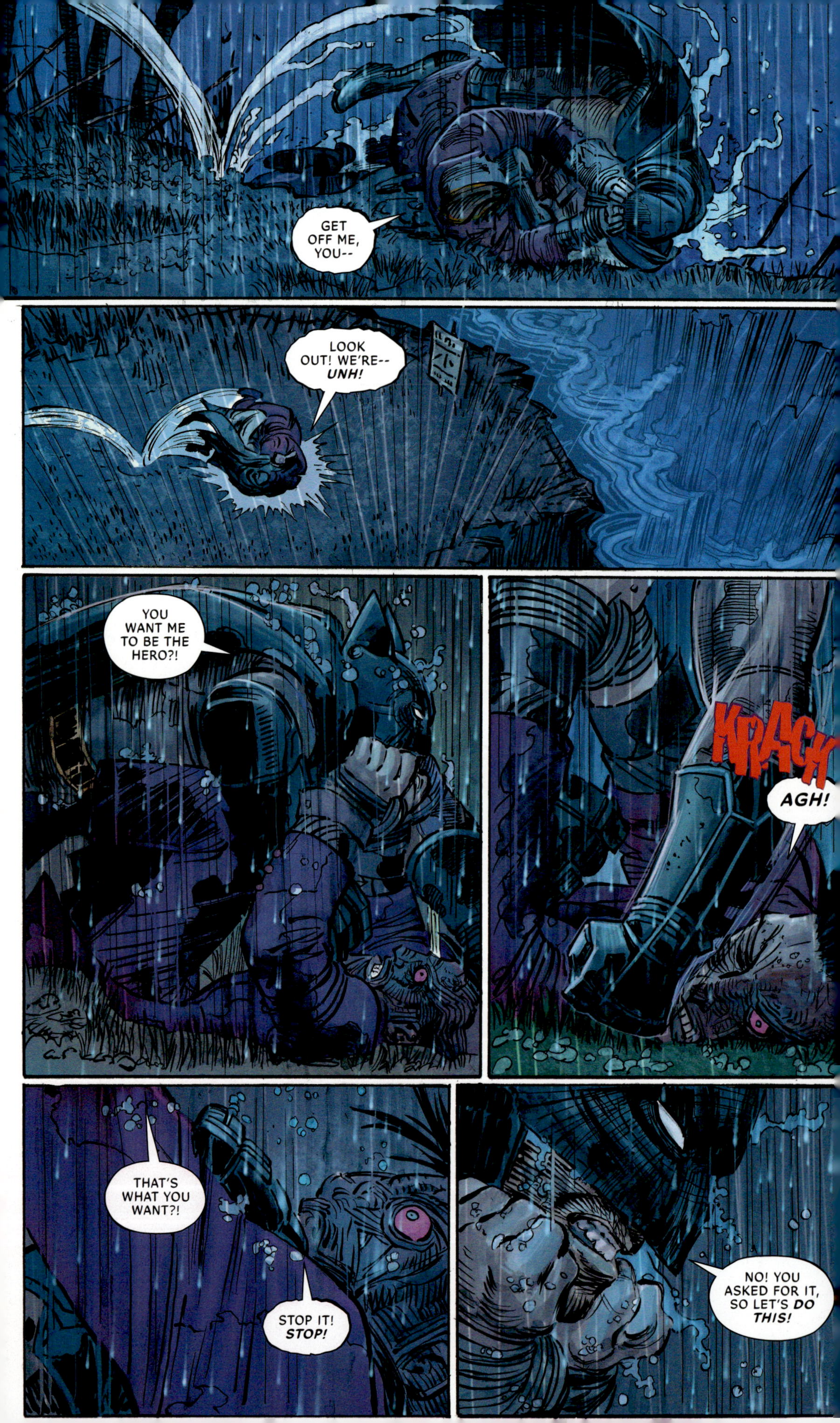

GET OFF ME, YOU--

LOOK OUT! WE'RE-- ***UNH!***

YOU WANT ME TO BE THE HERO?!

KRACK

AGH!

YES, DO IT, BRUCE!
DO IT!

BATMAN! DON'T DO IT! NOT THIS WAY! I CAN'T LET YOU!

DO IT!
DO IT!

THUNK

UNH...
HEH. WELL. I ACTUALLY DIDN'T THINK YOU HAD IT IN YOU, BATS... BUT LOOK AT THIS.

THE CLOUDS. BEFORE YOU DISAPPEAR, HARVEY, KILL THE CLOUDS OVER GOTHAM. NOW.

OF COURSE, BRUCE.

"AND THANK YOU."

"YEAH, THANKS, BATS. IT'S THE START OF A NEW ERA..."

I CAN FEEL IT, THE CURE...
I FEEL IT, TOO... IT...

IT FEELS...
...WRONG.

WHAT DID YOU DO?
WHAT DID YOU DO?!
NOTHING'S HAPPENING!
HE'S RIGHT! THE CURE ISN'T WORKING!
I WAS GOING TO DO IT, HARVEY. I WAS.
BUT WHAT I JUST GAVE YOU WASN'T YOUR CURE. IT WAS SOMETHING I MADE WITH HAROLD. A BOOSTER.
I ONLY BROUGHT IT BECAUSE I WAS WORRIED THAT WHATEVER YOU'D MADE HERE MIGHT NOT BE COMPLETE, OR WORSE, THAT TWO-FACE MIGHT HAVE CORRUPTED IT WITHOUT YOU KNOWING.
THE BOOSTER BONDS WITH NEURO-ACIDS AND *ILTS THEM POSITIVELY.* IF I'D ONDED IT TO YOUR CURE, THE COMPOUND MIGHT'VE TURNED YOU INTO HARVEY FOR GOOD. BUT YOUR CURE IS *HERE,* HARVEY, IN MY HAND.
AND TAKEN ALONE, THE BOOSTER *IMMUNIZES* THE BRAIN TO THOSE SAME ACIDS, MAKING IT IMPOSSIBLE FOR THEM TO AFFECT OR ALTER YOUR NEUROLOGY... *EVER.*
NO... NO, YOU DIDN'T...
AME HERE TO SAVE MY FRIEND, JT SEEING WHAT YOU'D MADE, EARNING WHAT YOU'D DONE... HE'S NOT HERE. NOT IN THIS PLACE.
SO FROM NOW ON, YOU'LL BE *HARVEY* IF YOU BATTLE HARDER TO BE HARVEY. OR *TWO-FACE* IF HE BATTLES HARDER. AND THAT'S HOW IT'LL BE. *PERMANENTLY.*

NO... NO...
YES, SO FIGHT, HARVEY. BECAUSE MAYBE TWO-FACE IS RIGHT. MAYBE HE *IS* STRONGER. MAYBE WE'RE ***ALL*** UGLIER INSIDE THAN I WANT TO ADMIT. MAYBE IT'S OUR NATURAL STATE. BUT IF THAT'S TRUE...WE JUST HAVE TO FIGHT HARDER.

NO...
I WAS WRONG TO TRY TO WIN THAT FIGHT FOR YOU. BECAUSE THE HARD TRUTH IS THAT THERE IS NO WINNING IT. NOT FOR YOU OR ME, OR ANYONE. EVER. THAT'S WHAT YOUR TRIP SHOWED ME.
ALL I CAN DO IS TELL YOU THAT WHEN I LOOK AT YOU, I STILL SEE SOMEONE I BELIEVE IN. AND AS LONG AS YOU FIGHT, I WILL FIGHT BESIDE YOU. ALWAYS

OH, AND I ADDED A SEDATIVE, TOO.
N...

SEE YOU BACK IN GOTHAM, HARVEY.

DUKE, LET'S GO H--
AAAAARGHH!

HELLO, AGAIN.
BEAST, I--
NNNNGG!

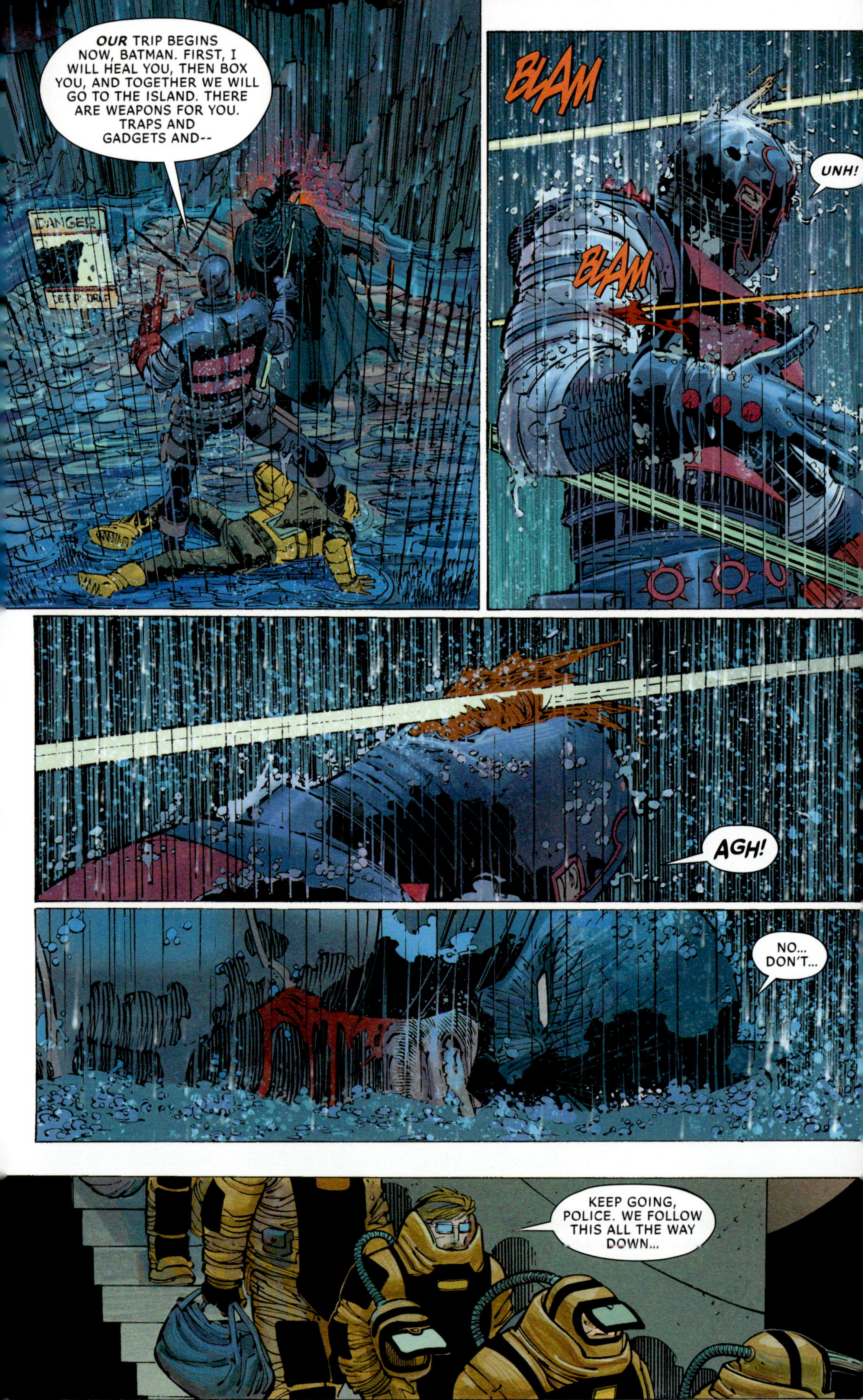

OUR TRIP BEGINS NOW, BATMAN. FIRST, I WILL HEAL YOU, THEN BOX YOU, AND TOGETHER WE WILL GO TO THE ISLAND. THERE ARE WEAPONS FOR YOU. TRAPS AND GADGETS AND--
DANGER
BLAM
UNH!
BLAM
AGH!
NO... DON'T...
KEEP GOING, POLICE. WE FOLLOW THIS ALL THE WAY DOWN...

GET AWAY FROM HIM. GET AWAY FROM BATMAN.
NOW. HE'S OURS.

GO! ≷COUGH COUGH≶...GET OUT OF HERE!

IT'S...IT'S THEM. BUT ARE THEY...

...HERE FOR MY PRIZE? OR AS MY PRIZE? BOTH?

BEAST... ≷UNH≶ DON'T HURT THEM...

OH BUT SEE THIS...THIS WILL BE A *TRUE* MESS. THE MESS PROMISED TO ME FROM THE START...
DANGER

WE SEE SOMETHING AHEAD, SIR!
KEEP GOING! TO THE END OF THIS THING!

I WON'T LET YOU!
BATMAN!
NO!
ARE THEY...?
LOOK!

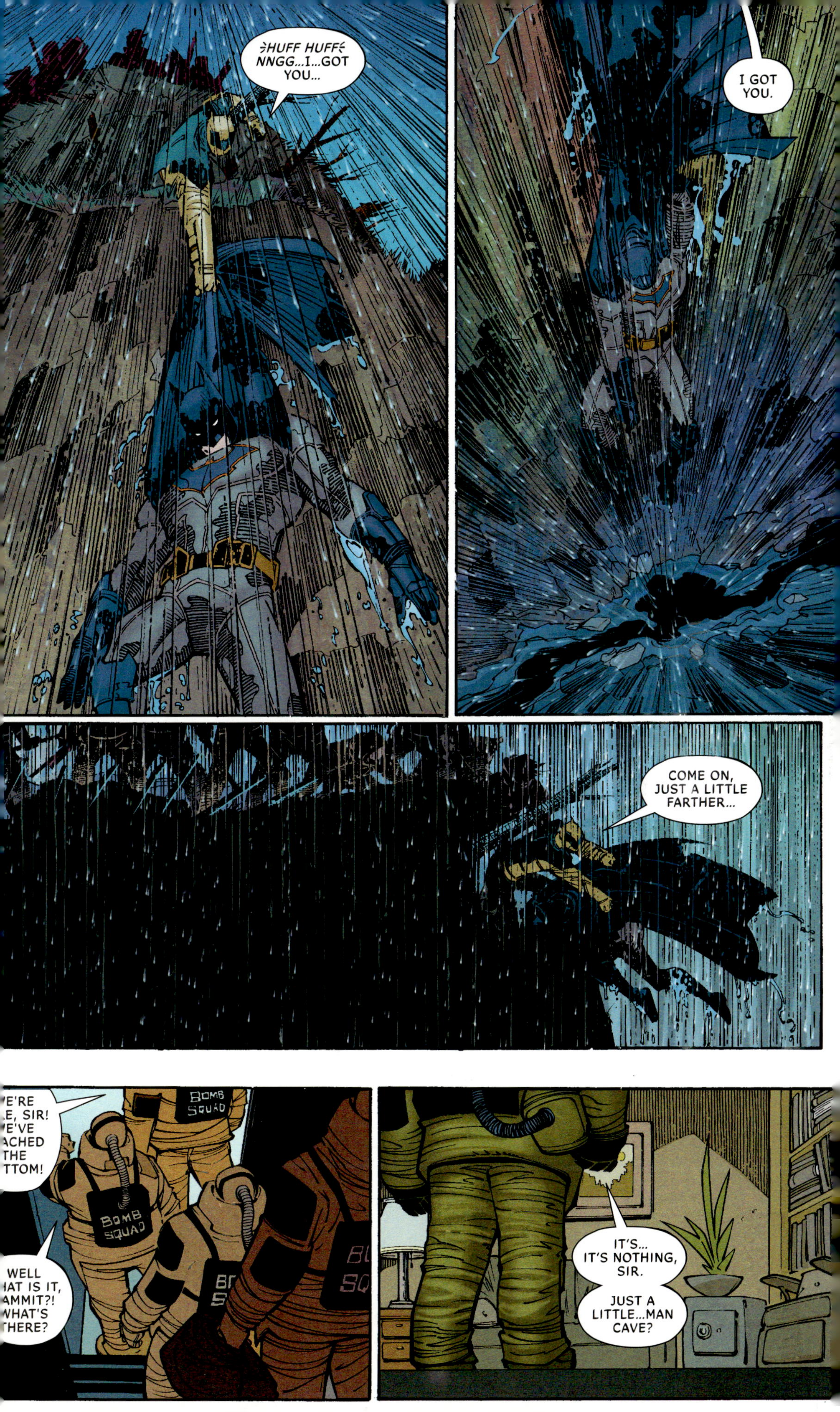

≶HUFF HUFF≶ NNGG...I...GOT YOU...

I GOT YOU.

COME ON, JUST A LITTLE FARTHER...

OR A PANIC ROOM. OR, WHATEVER. I TOLD YOU. THIS WHOLE THING WAS A DAMN GOOSE CHASE.
BUT, SIR--
WHAT THE HELL DO YOU THINK, EDMONDS?

HE HAS SOME MECHANISM THAT TAKES YOU DOWN THE WRONG STAIRWELL IF YOU'RE NOT THE BATMAN?
SOMETHING HIS OWN BUTLER DOESN'T KNOW ABOUT? WE CAN CHECK. BUT I'M TELLING YOU...

"IT'S OVER."
BATMAN, GET UP. THEY'RE ALL AROUND US.
WE HAVE TO FIGHT. BATMAN!

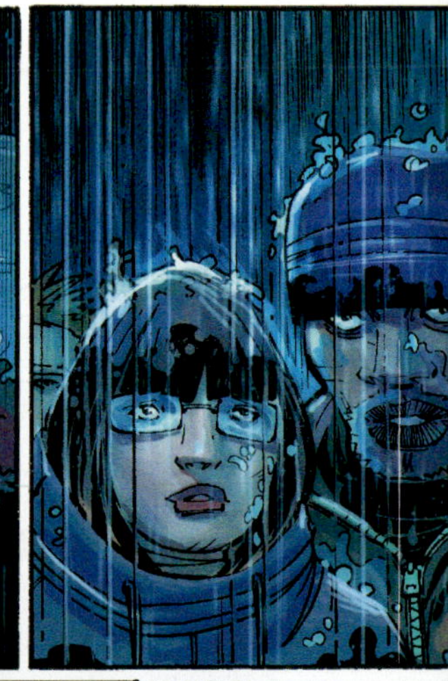

CAN YOU FIGHT?
NO... *COUGH* BUT I BET...I BET THEY'LL LET US PASS.

BATMAN.
THEY WILL. THEY'LL LET US PASS.
...ALL RIGHT.
COUGH AND THE COIN...

I WAS JUS ABOUT TO TH IT. YOU WA TO DO TH HONORS?
NO... NO, I WAS GOING TO SAY KEEP IT.

ALL RIGHT. *UGH* I WILL. BUT JUST FOR THE TOLLS.

"FAIR ENOUGH. AFTER ALL IT'S A LONG WAY HOME."
MILES TRAVELED: 0 MILES TO GO: 498

MY OWN WORST
ENEMY
FINALE
SCOTT SNYDER SCRIPT
JOHN ROMITA JR. PENCILS
DANNY MIKI, TOM PALMER,
SANDRA HOPE & RICHARD FRIEND INKS
DEAN WHITE COLORS
STEVE WANDS LETTERS
ROMITA, MIKI, WHITE COVER
DAVE WIELGOSZ ASSISTANT EDITOR
REBECCA TAYLOR ASSOCIATE EDITOR
MARK DOYLE EDITOR

MONTHS, 2 WEEKS AND 2 DAYS LATER.
I'M JUST SAYING, THERE ARE PERKS TO BEING UNDERGROUND, TOO. OUR LEGEND--
DING DONG
WHO THE HELL IS IT?!
ROMAN?
NO ONE, IT'S JUST--
MESS!
THE BACK! WAUGH! THE PASSAGE! GOGOGO!
WINK
END

IGNORE THE QUESTION AND DO IT.

IT'S YOUR FIRST CASE TOGETHER, DUKE. YOU AND HIM--YES, **HIM.** NOT YOU AND YOUR FRIENDS. NOT YOU IN YOUR HOMEMADE HELMET AND GLUED-ON PATCH.

"MOVE," HE SAYS IN THAT VOICE.

SO YOU DO.

BUT ALL THE WHILE, IN YOUR HEAD, YOU KEEP ASKING **THAT SAME** QUESTION. THE REAL QUESTION.

THE ONE YOU SEE IN THE EYES OF EVERYONE WHO SEES **YOU** NEXT TO **HIM**...

I WON'T ASK THE QUESTION. BUT THE ANSWER TO IT? BEST I CAN FIGURE?

HE'S #$%^&! CRAZY.
The Cursed Wheel Part 1
SCOTT SNYDER script DECLAN SHALVEY pencils & inks
JORDIE BELLAIRE colors STEVE WANDS letters
REBECCA TAYLOR associate editor MARK DOYLE editor

CHECK THEM. NOW.
NO PULSE.
NOTHING. JIM AND MEDICAL ARE EN ROUTE.

NO...
NO. FASTER. C.O.D. IS...?
THEY BLED TO DEATH. THE CUTS ARE SURGICAL. PARALLEL.
LOOK CLOSER.
DAMN.
IT'S A STYLE OF TORTURE KNOWN AS "STILLING." THE CUTS ARE SO CLOSE TOGETHER THAT ANY MOVEMENT TO CLOSE ONE CUT OPENS ANOTHER. YOUR BEST CHANCE AT SURVIVING IS STAYING STILL, WAITING FOR HELP.
BEST GUESS IS ZSASZ. THE KNIFE-WORK. SADISM.
I.D. IS COMING UP THAT THEY'RE ALL IMPORTERS. HIGH-END FABRICS. NO RECORDS ON ANY OF THEM.
SO GO ON. ASK THE QUESTION. THE ONLY ONE IN YOUR HEAD RIGHT NOW.
SIGH ALL RIGHT...

2 DAYS EARLIER.
"WHY YOU?"

BECAUSE I'M TRYING SOMETHING DIFFERENT, DUKE. LOOK.
I *AM.* WHAT AM I LOOKING AT?
THE NEXT YEAR OF YOUR LIFE.
LOOK, I TOLD YOU, IF YOU'RE TAKING ME IN BECAUSE OF MY *PARENTS,* BECAUSE YOU FEEL GUILTY OR SORRY FOR ME, JUST STOP. I'M FINE ON MY OWN. AND ROBIN TODAY, ROBIN DOESN'T *NEED* A BATMAN.
GOOD. BATMAN DOESN'T NEED A *ROBIN* EITHER.
THERE, ON THAT SCREEN, IS SOMETHING FOR WHICH I HAVE NO NAME. ALFRED CALLS IT--

THE "CURSED WHEEL." EMPHASIS ON CURSED.
THERE ARE TIMES I WISH I'D NEVER TAUGHT YOU WHAT I'D LEARNED.
IT'S A CONDENSED VERSION OF ALL MY TRAINING, ALL MY YEARS ABROAD, BUT SHARPENED, APPLIED TO TENETS TAUGHT TO ME BY ALFRED. TENETS ABOUT THE DEEPEST ASPECTS OF HUMAN IDENTITY. EVERY PART OF THE WHEEL IS DESIGNED TO TEST A DIFFERENT PART OF YOUR PSYCHOLOGY.
I'M NOT LOOKING TO BE A SIDEKICK, BRUCE. I--
IT'S NOT THE TRAINING TO BE A "SIDEKICK". IT'S THE TRAINING THAT COMES NEXT. EVERY ALLY WHO'S TRAINED WITH ME HAS GONE THROUGH IT.
WHETHER THEY KNOW IT OR NOT.
IT'S WHAT COMES AT THE END. WHAT MAKES YOU WHO YOU ARE. THE HERO YOU'LL BECOME.
OR EVEN THE VILLAIN.
VILLAIN...?
...JASON?
NO.
SOMEONE... ELSE.
IT DOESN'T MATTER. LOOK AT THE COLORS.

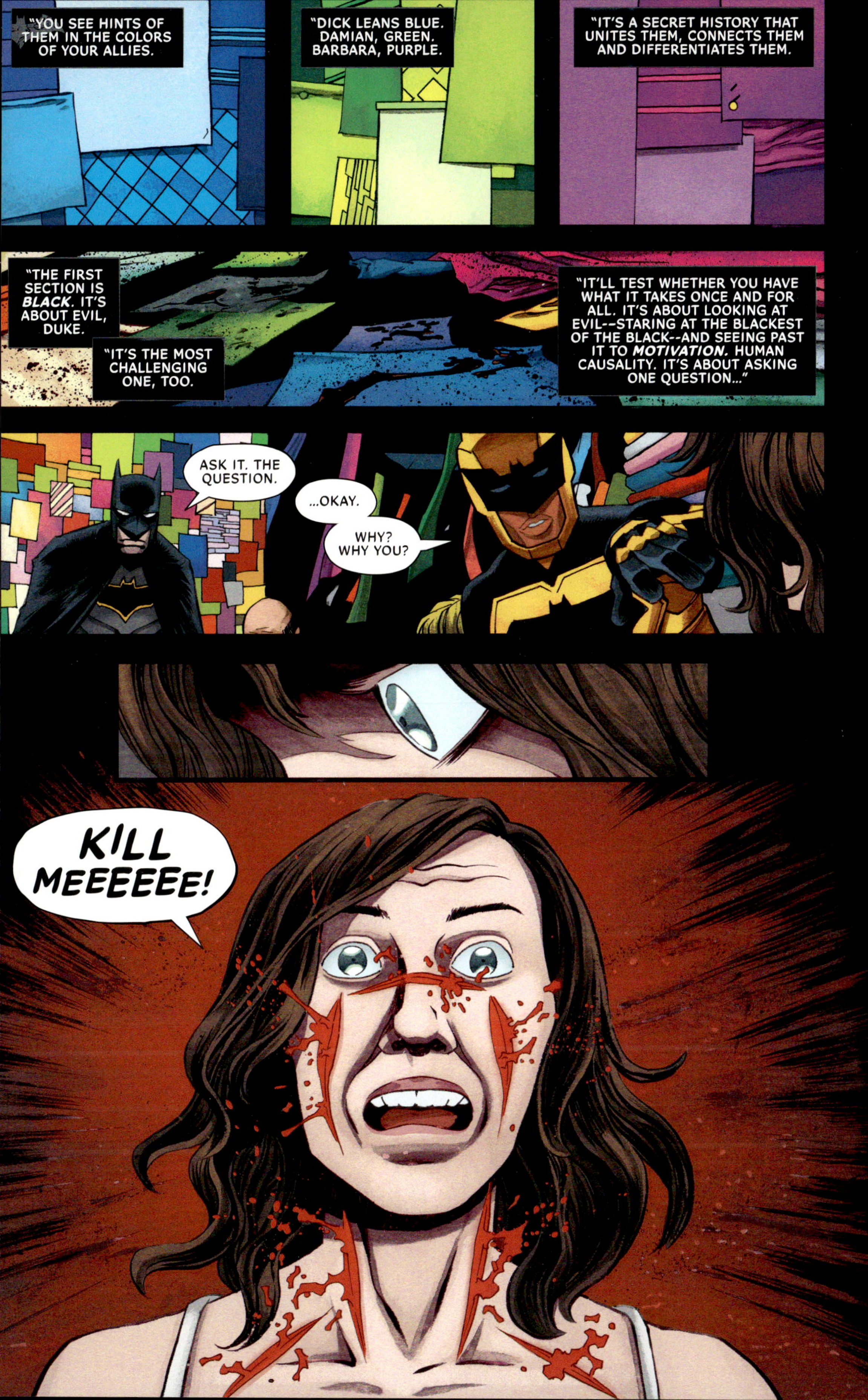

"YOU SEE HINTS OF THEM IN THE COLORS OF YOUR ALLIES.

"DICK LEANS BLUE. DAMIAN, GREEN. BARBARA, PURPLE.

"IT'S A SECRET HISTORY THAT UNITES THEM, CONNECTS THEM AND DIFFERENTIATES THEM.

ASK IT. THE QUESTION.

...OKAY.

WHY? WHY YOU?

KILL MEEEEEE!

"THIS IS ME...
"THIS IS MY FACE.
"BUT IT'S ALSO *YOUR* FACE."
The Cursed Wheel Part 2
SCOTT SNYDER script DECLAN SHALVEY pencils & inks
JORDIE BELLAIRE colors STEVE WANDS letters
REBECCA TAYLOR associate editor MARK DOYLE editor

"THIS IS THE DAY YOU AND DAD BROUGHT ME TO OUR APARTMENT IN TRACY TOWERS. THE SAME ONE YOU STILL LIVE IN.
"MY NINTH BIRTHDAY. I GOT FREAKED OUT ON THE TUNNEL OF LOVE AND TRIED TO CLIMB OUT, MOM. I HAD ONE LEG IN THE WATER, YOU REMEMBER?
"AND THIS IS YOU LEAVING FOR A CASE. YOU'RE A SOCIAL WORKER, MOM. YOU REMEMBER?
"YOU HELP KIDS FROM THE NARROWS GET BACK ON TRACK. YOU'VE WORKED WITH SOME OF THE *TOUGH* CASES.
"THE MORNING IN THE PICTURE, YOU WERE GOING TO MEET WITH A UKRAINIAN BOY WHO WAS RUMORED TO BE ONE OF THE MOST PROLIFIC *KILLERS* FOR THE DEVIL PIGS. YOU REMEMBER?
"THE BOY CLAIMED TO BE INNOCENT, SAID THAT THE GANG WAS PINNING THE KILLINGS ON HIM. YOU WENT TO MEET HIM TO FIND OUT.
"HE WAS MY AGE AT THE TIME. THIRTEEN YEARS OLD.
"I REMEMBER I WAS JUST STARTING TO UNDERSTAND WHAT YOU DID FOR A LIVING, AND I ASKED YOU HOW YOU'D KNOW. HOW YOU'D KNOW IF THE BOY WAS REALLY GOOD, OR BAD.
"AND YOU TOLD ME YOU HAD A RULE. THAT WHEN YOU WEREN'T SURE ABOUT SOMEONE, YOU MET THEM FIRST THING IN THE *MORNING,* IN THE NEW LIGHT, YOU SAID. PEOPLE HAVE A HARDER TIME *HIDING* WHO THEY ARE FIRST THING IN THE MORNING.
THAT'S YOU.

THAT'S YOU, MOM. GOING OUT BY LIGHT OF DAY TO DO GOOD IN THE WORLD. FIRST THING IN THE MORNING.
THAT'S YOU.
YOU...YOU KNOW WHO YOU ARE?
YOU'RE A ROTTEN NOTHING.
YOU'RE A PITY CASSSSSSE.
HE TOOK YOU IN OUT OF GUILT. HE TOOK YOU IN WHEN YOU'VE GOT NOTHING GOING FOR YOU...
BUT YOOOUUUUU... YOU'RE ANOTHER EMPTY SIDEKICKKKK.
STOP IT. MOM, IT'S ME, PLEASE--
I KNOW IT'S YOU. I'M ASHAMED OF YOU, DUKE. I HATE YOU.
I'LL KILL YOU.
I'LL KILL YOU!
LOOK AT THIS. THIS IS ME. THIS IS YOU. I LOVE YOU.
I HATE YOU! I'LLLLL KILLLL YOUUUUU!
STOP!
HAHA! KILLLLLLL!
STOP IT! STOP!
STOP!

BTERRANEAN THROUGHWAY TO GOTHAM.
WORK IN PROGRESS.
ZSASZ. HE PICKS PEOPLE WHO HAVE A LOT TO LIVE FOR. WHO LOVE LIFE. HE SETS HIS SIGHTS ON THEM, STALKS THEM, AND KILLS THEM PAINFULLY IN FRONT OF EACH OTHER.
IT'S RARE THAT SOMEONE ESCAPES HIM. BUT WHEN THEY DO, HE WILL NOT STOP UNTIL HE FINDS THEM. HE RESERVES SOME OF THE **WORST** PAIN HE DOLES OUT FOR THE ONES WHO ESCAPED.
IN THE FABRIC WAREHOUSE, THERE WAS ONE VICTIM, NOT OUR SURVIVOR, BUT A DECEASED, **RITA NOLES,** WHO WAS CUT MORE PAINFULLY THAN THE REST. SHE WAS GIVEN COAGULATES TO KEEP HER FROM BLEEDING OUT AS FAST.
SO HE PEGGED **NOLES** AS SOMEONE WHO'D ESCAPED HIM IN THE PAST?
ALFRED IS SEARCHING THE DATABASES TO SEE IF SHE WAS.
HE'S ALSO RUNNING A SEARCH ON OUR VICTIM, DIANA BOONE, THE WOMAN WE FOUND **ALIVE.**
HE'S RECOVERING THE HOSPITAL WITH AND A FULL DETAIL. LL SEE WHAT WE FIND HER HOUSE. BE CARE- L ON YOUR LEFT. THE ROAD WILL BEND WITH US.
ON IT. IS SHE GOING TO LIVE?
IT'S UNCLEAR. BUT DUKE, WITH THIS CASE, LOOK PAST THE EVIL TO THE **MOTIVATION,** TO THE THREADS OF CAUSAL BEHAVIOR THAT ALLOW YOU TO SOLVE THINGS. THAT'S WHERE YOU ARE IN THE WHEEL.
SEE PAST THE WHOLE TO THE PIECES...

FROM WHAT WE'VE GATHERED, OUR SURVIVOR, MS. BOONE, LIVED ALONE. SHE SPECIALIZED IN HIGH-END FABRIC IMPORTATION. HER BUSINESS IS ON THE RISE.
THE OTHERS AT THAT WAREHOUSE, THOUGH...THE CHECKS ON THOSE IMPORTERS. NEARLY ALL OF THEM ARE UNDER INVESTIGATION FOR TRANSPORTING ILLEGAL SUBSTANCES INSIDE DOMESTIC AND INTERNATIONAL SHIPMENTS.
SO SHE RAN WITH A BAD CROWD. YOU THINK ONE OF THEM SET ZSASZ ON NOLES? OUR VICTIM JUST GOT CAUGHT IN THE MIX? SURVIVED BY LUCK?
I'LL CHECK UPSTAIR YOU CHE DOWN
AGAIN WE'R LOOKIN FOR MOT SHE WA THE ON ONE TO L SO--
WHO SHE
NO BETTER PLACE TO START THAN IN THE BASEMENT.
KILL MEEEEEE!
I'LL KILL YOU!

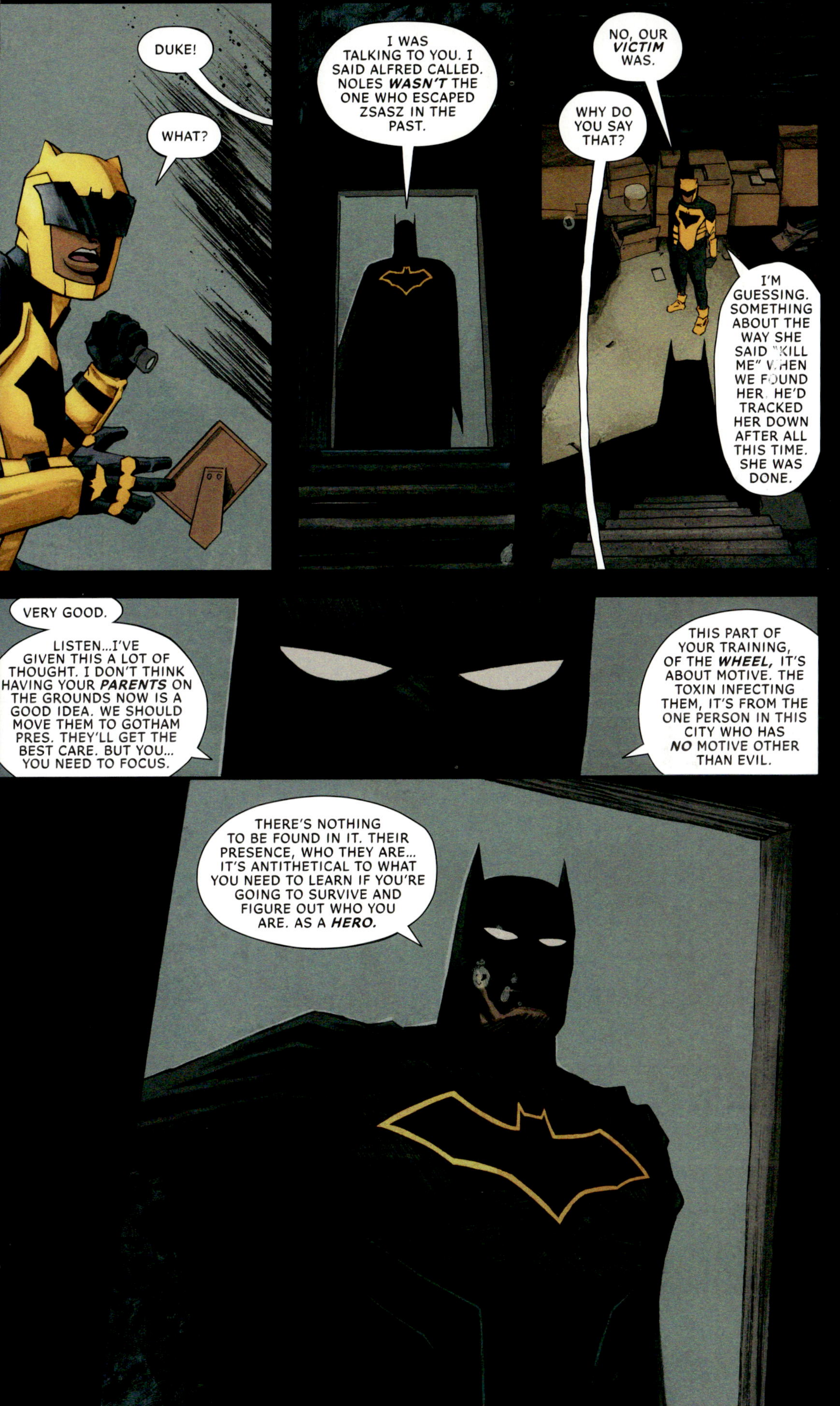
DUKE!
WHAT?
I WAS TALKING TO YOU. I SAID ALFRED CALLED. NOLES WASN'T THE ONE WHO ESCAPED ZSASZ IN THE PAST.
WHY DO YOU SAY THAT?
NO, OUR VICTIM WAS.
I'M GUESSING. SOMETHING ABOUT THE WAY SHE SAID "KILL ME" WHEN WE FOUND HER. HE'D TRACKED HER DOWN AFTER ALL THIS TIME. SHE WAS DONE.
VERY GOOD.
LISTEN...I'VE GIVEN THIS A LOT OF THOUGHT. I DON'T THINK HAVING YOUR PARENTS ON THE GROUNDS NOW IS A GOOD IDEA. WE SHOULD MOVE THEM TO GOTHAM PRES. THEY'LL GET THE BEST CARE. BUT YOU... YOU NEED TO FOCUS.
THIS PART OF YOUR TRAINING, OF THE WHEEL, IT'S ABOUT MOTIVE. THE TOXIN INFECTING THEM, IT'S FROM THE ONE PERSON IN THIS CITY WHO HAS NO MOTIVE OTHER THAN EVIL.
THERE'S NOTHING TO BE FOUND IN IT. THEIR PRESENCE, WHO THEY ARE... IT'S ANTITHETICAL TO WHAT YOU NEED TO LEARN IF YOU'RE GOING TO SURVIVE AND FIGURE OUT WHO YOU ARE. AS A HERO.

MAYBE THERE'S NOTHING TO FIGURE OUT. MAYBE I'M NOT A HERO AT ALL. MAYBE I'M JUST SOME KID WHO'S RUN HIS COURSE WITH THIS STUFF. MAYBE YOU JUST TOOK ME IN OUT OF GUILT AND THIS WHOLE THING...IT'S ABOUT YOU. SOME MOTIVE YOU HAVE.
MAYBE.
Sigh
WHO ARE YOU?
SHE'S A MARK.
LIKE YOU.
WHAT THE--?!

AND I KNOW JUST WHERE YOU GO.

The Cursed Wheel

Part 3

SCOTT SNYDER
script
DECLAN SHALVEY
pencils & inks

JORDIE BELLAIRE
colors
STEVE WANDS
letters
REBECCA TAYLOR
associate editor
MARK DOYLE
editor

CLEAR UP!

THEN.

NOW.
IT WAS A SIMPLE MISTAKE, DUKE. YOU'LL GET BETTER.
THANKS, BRUCE.
AND ZSASZ?
HE'S OUT THERE, BUT WE'LL GET HIM.
IT SEEMS WE HAVE A REASON THAT ZSASZ MISTOOK RITA NOLES FOR OUR SURVIVOR, DIANA BOONE. BOONE OFTEN WORE CLOTHES MADE FROM THE *CORALS* SHE IMPORTED.
ON THE NIGHT IN QUESTION, NOLES SPILLED WINE ON HER BLOUSE. BORROWED ONE FROM BOONE. ZSASZ ENTERED, MISTOOK NOLES FOR BOONE, THE WOMAN WHO'D *ESCAPED* HIM AS A GIRL.
SO OUR SURVIVOR, BOONE...SHE JUST LUCKED INTO SURVIVING BECAUSE ZSASZ DIDN'T RECOGNIZE HER IN THE DARK, IN HIS FRENZY. ALL BECAUSE THE TWO WOMEN LOOKED ALIKE. NO REASON BUT PLAIN CRUEL LUCK.
MAYBE, MAYBE NOT. GET SOME REST.

BRUCE.
I WAS THINKING. YOU CAN PUT THE CALL THROUGH. MOVE MY FOLKS OUT.
...
ALL RIGHT.
IT'S MORNING. TIME TO SLEEP.
WILL DO.
NO.
SCREW THIS.

HERE YOU GO, MS. BOONE. I'LL GET YOUR THINGS FROM HOLDING.
THANK YOU, OFFICER. I JUST WANT MY PHONE. I WAS HOPING TO...I DON'T KNOW...
REMIND YOURSELF THE WORLD IS OUT THERE? I GET IT. HANG IN THERE.
THANKS...
DIANA BOONE. WHY YOU?
WHY THIS WAY?
THE BEST CHANCE TO SEE IT IS NOW, DUKE. IN THE LIGHT OF DAY.
SO LOOK.

'T CAN'T BE THAT YOU RVIVED ZSASZ TWICE BY CIDENT, DIANA. THAT HE AS AFTER YOU BUT GOT TA NOLES INSTEAD, ALL JST BECAUSE OF SOME ANDOM SCREWUP, AND V HE'S STILL OUT THERE HUNTING YOU...
THINGS CAN'T ALL BE THAT RANDOM.
SO LOOK, DUKE.
COME ON. FIND IT...FIND THE REASON. FIND YOUR...
...ANSWER?
THE CLOTHES...
...THE ONES YOU WORE TO THE MEETING, DIANA...
...THEY'RE THE WRONG ONES.

THE ONES YOU WORE TO THE MEETING, THEY'RE NOT CORAL FABRIC. THEY'RE NOT YOUR COLOR. ZSASZ MISTOOK RITA NOLES FOR YOU BECAUSE SHE WAS WEARING A BLOUSE YOU GAVE HER.
YOU CAUSED IT, DIANA, DIDN'T YOU? YOU'RE THE--
...
DAMMIT!
HELP! HELP ME!
WAKE UP, KID! WAKE UP!
"I SAID WAKE UP."

THEN.
DUKE. BABY BIRD?
WHAT IS IT, MOM?
I...I LIED TO YOU EARLIER. THAT BOY. HE WAS GUILTY. HE KILLED OVER A DOZEN PEOPLE. I SAW IT RIGHT AWAY, JUST...SOMETIMES I DON'T WANT THAT TO BE THE WORLD YOU LIVE IN. THAT'S ALL.
OKAY. *YAWN*
Heh. GO TO BED, BABY BIRD. IT'S DARK OUT...
...TIME TO SLEEP.

IGNORE IT ALL, DUKE.
IGNORE EVERYTHING BUT THE QUESTION.
THE ONE IT ALL COMES BACK TO.
AND ASK IT.
ASK HER.

WHY?
GO AWAY! LEAVE ME ALONE!
MS. BOONE. STOP.
STAY BACK!
ALL RIGHT. JUST CALM DOWN.
YOU DON'T UNDERSTAND... I CHANGED MY NAME, MY FACE... I WAS *TERRIFIED* HE'D FIND ME ONE DAY. WHEN I HEARD HE WAS OUT, I...IT WAS ALL A MISTAKE...
IT WAS...

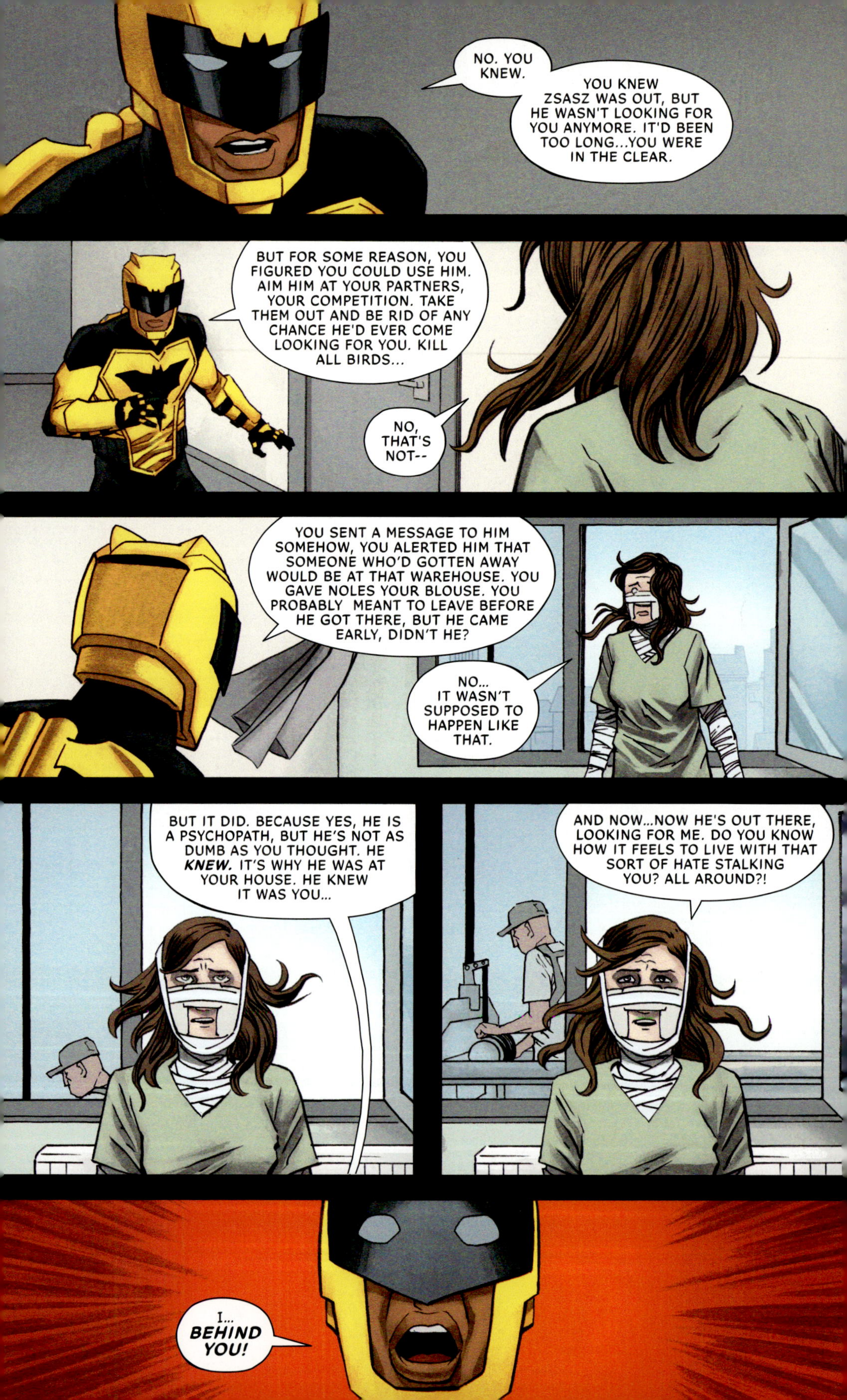
NO. YOU KNEW.
YOU KNEW ZSASZ WAS OUT, BUT HE WASN'T LOOKING FOR YOU ANYMORE. IT'D BEEN TOO LONG...YOU WERE IN THE CLEAR.
BUT FOR SOME REASON, YOU FIGURED YOU COULD USE HIM. AIM HIM AT YOUR PARTNERS, YOUR COMPETITION. TAKE THEM OUT AND BE RID OF ANY CHANCE HE'D EVER COME LOOKING FOR YOU. KILL ALL BIRDS...
NO, THAT'S NOT--
YOU SENT A MESSAGE TO HIM SOMEHOW, YOU ALERTED HIM THAT SOMEONE WHO'D GOTTEN AWAY WOULD BE AT THAT WAREHOUSE. YOU GAVE NOLES YOUR BLOUSE. YOU PROBABLY MEANT TO LEAVE BEFORE HE GOT THERE, BUT HE CAME EARLY, DIDN'T HE?
NO... IT WASN'T SUPPOSED TO HAPPEN LIKE THAT.
BUT IT DID. BECAUSE YES, HE IS A PSYCHOPATH, BUT HE'S NOT AS DUMB AS YOU THOUGHT. HE *KNEW.* IT'S WHY HE WAS AT YOUR HOUSE. HE KNEW IT WAS YOU...
AND NOW...NOW HE'S OUT THERE, LOOKING FOR ME. DO YOU KNOW HOW IT FEELS TO LIVE WITH THAT SORT OF HATE STALKING YOU? ALL AROUND?!
I... **BEHIND YOU!**

ZSASZ!
NO!

THERE YOU ARE, LITTLE MARK. I HAVE A PLACE FOR YOU...
I HAVE A PLACE ON THE BACK OF MY HEAD WHERE I WILL NOT SEE Y--

THEY SLEEP DURING THE DAY MOSTLY. THEY LOOK ALMOST PEACEFUL, DON'T THEY?
...
I WANTED TO LET YOU KNOW, I JUST GOT WORD THAT *TWO-FACE* MIGHT BE BACK IN TOWN. HE'S LIKELY HOW DIANA BOONE GOT A MESSAGE TO *ZSASZ,* AND WHY SHE DID...
...WITH HIM IN TOWN, NO SECRET IS SAFE.
SHE FIGURED, TAKE OUT HER PARTNERS BEFORE THEY LET HER STATUS AS A TARGET OF ZSASZ LEAK. MAKE HER DEAL WITH TWO-FACE.
THAT'S PRETTY COLD.
YOU SAW IT, THOUGH...
...LIKE *SHE* WOULD HAVE.
THANKS, BRUCE.
BUT THE NURSES AREN'T COMING.

WHAT?
I WANT MY PARENTS TO STAY.
DUKE, THE VENOM IN THEM IS FROM THE *JOKER.* THE JOKER IS PURE EVIL, AND--
NO, HE'S NOT. HE'S YOUR BLIND SPOT.
WHAT?
YOU THINK JOKER IS JUST EVIL, JUST *PURE BLACK,* BUT HE'S NOT. HE ATTACKS WHAT HE LOVES. HIS SERUM MAKES VICTIMS DO THE SAME. SO MY *PARENTS?* EVERY HORRIBLE THING OUT OF THEIR MOUTHS? THEY'RE ACTUALLY TELLING ME HOW MUCH THEY LOVE ME.
THAT'S THE *MOTIVATION* BEHIND THE BLACKNESS. SO PLEASE, LET THEM STAY. I CAN TAKE IT.
ALL RIGHT THEN. I WILL. IF YOU ASK THE QUESTION...THE ONE I CAN SEE IS ON YOUR MIND.
OKAY. I WILL...

The Cursed Wheel Part 4

SCOTT SNYDER script DECLAN SHALVEY pencils & inks
JORDIE BELLAIRE colors STEVE WANDS letters
REBECCA TAYLOR associate editor MARK DOYLE editor

ALL★STAR
BATMAN
VARIANT COVER GALLERY

ALL-STAR BATMAN #1 variant by JOCK

ALL-STAR BATMAN #2 variant by JOCK

ALL-STAR BATMAN #3 variant by JOCK

ALL-STAR BATMAN #4 variant by JOCK

ALL-STAR BATMAN #5 variant by JOCK
Jock

ALL-STAR BATMAN #1 variant by DECLAN SHALVEY and JORDIE BELLAIRE

ALL-STAR BATMAN #2 variant by DECLAN SHALVEY and JORDIE BELLAIRE

ALL-STAR BATMAN #3 variant by DECLAN SHALVEY and JORDIE BE[illegible]RE

ALL-STAR BATMAN #4 variant by DECLAN SHALVEY and JORDIE BELLAIRE

ALL-STAR BATMAN #5 variant by DECLAN SHALVEY and JORDIE BELLAIRE

ALL-STAR BATMAN #1 variant
by NEAL ADAMS and HI-FI

ALL-STAR BATMAN #1 variant by LEE BERMEJO

ALL-STAR BATMAN #1 variant by BEN CALDWELL

ALL-STAR BATMAN #1 variant by
TYLER KIRKHAM and TOMEU MOREY

ALL-STAR BATMAN #1 variant by BARRY KITSON

ALL-STAR BATMAN #1 variant by JAE LEE and JUNE CHUNG

ALL-STAR BATMAN #1 variant by GUILLEM MARCH

ALL-STAR BATMAN #1 variant by RODOLFO MIGLIARI

ALL-STAR BATMAN #1 variant by BEN OLIVER

ALL-STAR BATMAN #1 variant by AFUA RICHARDSON

ALL-STAR BATMAN #1 variant by
MICHAEL TURNER and PETER STEIGERWALD